International *A*⸻ and
*W*OLVES ⸻ ⸻ ⸻ ⸻ ON

"Yousef Al-Mohaimeed has written a remarkable, rhythmic, genuine novel, throbbing with sensuality and moral courage, as if it didn't take place in a society that denies the tick of the heart." —HANAN AL-SHAYKH, AUTHOR OF *WOMEN OF SAND AND MYRRH*

"A novel that draws you in from the very first lines and doesn't let go." —*AL-MUSTAQBAL* (BEIRUT)

"Gripping. . . . Al-Mohaimeed writes with fire [and] with words that cut through the barbed wire in search of the dawn." —*MARIANNE* (PARIS)

"An exceptional work of imagination and writing." —*AL-RIYADH* (RIYADH)

"Beguiling. . . . Tightly engineered. . . . A startlingly pointed insider's lament over the daily, anonymous brutalities of modern Saudi society. . . . It is literally the oldest story in the world. But in Al-Mohaimeed's capable hands, it is imbued with new life. . . . The story's brisk pace is well served by Anthony Calderbank's clean, free-flowing translation."

—*THE DAILY STAR* (BEIRUT)

"[*Wolves of the Crescent Moon*] could be read like a variation on Sartre's hellish *No Exit*. . . . With a blistering style . . . but with no pamphleteering, Al-Mohaimeed describes the Arab inferno."

—LE NOUVEL OBSERVATEUR (PARIS)

"A gripping story. . . . More powerful and deeper than one would imagine, given its brevity. . . . Compelling."

—THE JORDAN TIMES

"[*Wolves of the Crescent Moon*] proves irresistible in terms of the pleasures of a discovery. . . . [Al-Mohaimeed] tears the masks from and lands a resounding slap in the faces of the pious and hypocritical, by shedding luminous daylight upon the evils of a masochistic and homophobic society, cloaked in the affectations of a feigned religiosity."

—EVENE (PARIS)

"Deeply moving. . . . Unsettling and controversial."

—DAILY NEWS EGYPT

PENGUIN BOOKS

WOLVES OF THE CRESCENT MOON

Yousef Al-Mohaimeed was born in Riyadh in 1964. He has published several novels and short story collections in Arabic; *Wolves of the Crescent Moon* is his first book to be published outside the Middle East. In 2004 Al-Mohaimeed was presented with an award by *Diwan al Arab* magazine and the Egyptian Journalists Union in recognition of his creative contribution to Arab culture. He lives in Riyadh.

Anthony Calderbank is the translator of Nobel laureate Naguib Mahfouz's novel *Rhadopis of Nubia*, Sonallah Ibrahim's *Zaat*, and Miral al-Tahawy's *The Tent* and *Blue Aubergine*. He lives in Khobar, Saudi Arabia.

WOLVES OF THE CRESCENT MOON

A NOVEL

Yousef Al-Mohaimeed

Translated from the Arabic by
Anthony Calderbank

PENGUIN BOOKS

Published by the Penguin Group
Penguin Group (USA) Inc., 375 Hudson Street, New York, New York 10014, U.S.A. •
Penguin Group (Canada), 90 Eglinton Avenue East, Suite 700, Toronto, Ontario, Canada
M4P 2Y3 (a division of Pearson Penguin Canada Inc.) • Penguin Books Ltd, 80 Strand,
London WC2R 0RL, England • Penguin Ireland, 25 St Stephen's Green, Dublin 2, Ireland (a
division of Penguin Books Ltd) • Penguin Books (Australia), 250 Camberwell Road,
Camberwell, Victoria 3124, Australia (a division of Pearson Australia Group Pty Ltd) •
Penguin Books India Pvt Ltd, 11 Community Centre, Panchsheel Park, New Delhi – 110 017,
India • Penguin Group (NZ), 67 Apollo Drive, Rosedale, North Shore 0632, New Zealand (a
division of Pearson New Zealand Ltd) • Penguin Books (South Africa) (Pty) Ltd, 24 Sturdee
Avenue, Rosebank, Johannesburg 2196, South Africa

Penguin Books Ltd, Registered Offices:
80 Strand, London WC2R 0RL, England

First published in Egypt by the American University in Cairo Press 2007
Published in Penguin Books 2007

10 9 8 7 6 5 4 3 2 1

Originally published in Arabic in 2003 as *Fikhakh al-ra'iha* by Riyadh al-Rayyis, Beirut.

An earlier version of two chapters, "A Body Like Ripe Fruit" and "Stolen Manhood,"
appeared in *Banipal* (London), no. 20, Summer 2004.

Publisher's Note
This is a work of fiction. Names, characters, places, and incidents either are the product of
the author's imagination or are used fictitiously, and any resemblance to actual persons,
living or dead, business establishments, events, or locales is entirely coincidental.

LIBRARY OF CONGRESS CATALOGUING IN PUBLICATION DATA
Muhaymid, Yusuf.
[Fikhakh al-ra'ihah. English]
Wolves of the crescent moon / Yousef Al-Mohaimeed ; translated by Anthony Calderbank
p. cm.
ISBN 978-0-14-311321-8
1. Calderbank, Anthony. II. Title.
PJ7850.U4538F5513 2008
892.7'36—dc22   2007018030

Printed in the United States of America
Set in Village Roman • Designed by Sabrina Bowers

Contents

WOLVES OF THE CRESCENT MOON

Prologue

"WHERE TO?"

The young ticket clerk was busy sorting the banknotes into the till according to their denomination. When he heard no answer he raised his head and peered through the round opening in the glass at the man standing in front of him. White hairs twitched on the customer's chin, his eyes bulged slightly, and a thick mustache covered his upper lip.

Turad hadn't yet decided where he was going. He simply had entered the bus station and walked up to the ticket counter. He had come utterly to loathe this city and everyone in it. He had spent the last two nights sleeping in the basement of an old mosque. For two whole days he had been roaming the streets, wandering into gardens and *souks*, and rummaging through the shops, one after the other. It was as if to reassure himself he wouldn't be missing anything in particular by leaving the city that he had lived in for years, and that he had sought refuge in as a destitute and defenseless young man. Nights he had learned to read and write, spelling out the words letter by letter. During the days he had worked like a dog in the scorching heat, first as a day laborer, then as a tea boy; as a security guard in a bank, and as a guard at the gate of a palace; and finally as a messenger in a ministry. "To hell with this city and the people in it. They have stripped me of every ounce of dignity and decency. Are they Arabs or what?" Turad asked himself, as the ticket clerk repeated his question:

"Where to, sir?"

Good grief! Turad thought to himself. What did the boy say? He called me "sir." Yes. He certainly meant me. He was looking straight at me when he said "sir." You polite boy. Where did you come from? Don't call me "sir" or you'll make me change my mind about leaving this damn city. Perhaps if you saw the other boys, some of whom are even younger than you, tugging my *thobe* or kicking me on the backside; perhaps if you saw my left ear, which I always hide under the edge of my *shmagh*, you might change your mind and curse me in front of everybody. You might scream at me, "Fuck off, you old tramp!"

"Can you hear me, sir? Where do you wish to travel to?" The ticket clerk had lifted himself up off his seat and leaned his face toward the round hole in the glass.

"I don't know."

"Well, then, could you just take a seat over there in the waiting room until you've made up your mind? Look, there are other people behind you waiting their turn." After casting a quick glance at the long line building up behind him, Turad withdrew morosely and walked slowly over to the last row of seats in the waiting room. There was nothing beyond it except a huge glass wall. He sat and contemplated the street outside as things began to wind down for the night and the city rubbed its eyes sleepily, the yellow disk of the sun shimmering on the distant horizon.

There, in that vast ministry building, my feet had combed every corridor as I carried in my right hand the shiny brass coffeepot and three very small, ornately patterned china coffee cups. I'd stand at the door of the office, lift the pot up in the air, and pour. I used to take great pleasure in the task, moving from guest to guest with that coffee aroma perking them up. When the director of financial affairs gestured to me with his hand "enough," I would leave immediately. I hated his arrogance. I don't know why he treated me like that. Nevertheless, I put up with it and managed to control my anger and irritation so I could hang on to the job. I had lost my previous job guarding that huge gate. I had been very honest in my work; not a thing got past me. Then

I stopped the gentleman that the lady of the palace wanted let in. I'd stopped him because the master had warned me not to let in anyone I didn't know when he wasn't there. But then the damn master fired me without any explanation. Had the lady concocted some plot against me? Had she spoken falsely about me, or had she just looked for something to accuse me of? Was it because I spent too long looking at her women friends as they passed through the gate? If I did, I wasn't leering. It was only because I wanted to make sure of who they were before I let them in. I had to be sure they were really women and not men, because I didn't want any unsavory characters coming in. So it was without any reason or explanation that I found myself thrown into the street with nothing but my suitcase. Eventually I found the ministry and frittered away my life in its corridors, and in the tiny room for making tea and coffee.

After all roads tired of his wretched feet, and posh offices ejected him, and faces shunned him, after all the houses turned him away, he had decided to vie with the Indians and Bangladeshis washing cars. "There's nothing dishonorable about it," he told himself out loud, but the voice residing deep inside chastised him: "You, son of the free tribes, son of the wild lands and the wide canyons, how can you accept becoming a cleaner, a servant, or a slave?" "We are all His slaves," he would say to console himself.

From the parking lot outside the ministry he got his foot in the door of its offices, thanks to the intervention of the director of financial affairs, whose arrogance and abuse rained down on him every day even in front of his guests and clients. One day, around noon, the man yelled at him, "You oaf!" Turad lost his temper and threw the coffee on the floor, glaring at him with that noble and ferocious face he had left in the desert amid the springs and the wadis. He had thrown it away in the shifting sand beneath the *awshaz* trees that reel in the wind like genies' heads. Turad looked at him furiously. "I am not an oaf," he told him. "I am the son of a tribe. It is fate that has placed me here in front of you, and if I am an oaf, it is because I am working here with you." He said lots of things that had been bottled up inside for thirteen years. He left feeling greatly relieved, a huge burden lifted off his chest. In the end he returned again to the same ministry, thanks to the intervention of some of the staff, and he apologized to the director, who accepted on condition that he work as a messenger for the staff in the finance department.

Turad came to with a start as a voice over the loudspeaker announced the departure of bus number eight, and informed passengers that they should make their way immediately to the stand. He was watching the people milling around the door of the bus when he suddenly noticed, on the table in front of him, a glass of tea, its steam twisting into the air. The man who'd bought it hadn't had time to drink it and had left it there when he ran over to the bus in order to get a window seat. Turad stretched out his trembling hand and lifted the tea to his lips. He savored it gratefully, then wrapped his *shmagh* tightly around his face, which was turned to the glass wall behind him. He drew in a deep breath and contemplated the tower blocks and minarets as the city succumbed to darkness. Dear Lord, should I really be leaving the city, its people, its intimate mud houses, and its warm cozy alleys just because of what happened? Was I right to resign from my position? He laughed sarcastically. Could you call that job a position? Can the role of an entertainer or a clown dressed in a crumpled *thobe* be called a "position"? Once one of the fools tugged my *thobe* from behind. Another time one of them stuck his leg out between the desks and I fell flat on my face. So many times they'd try to pull off my *shmagh*, which I wrapped around my head. It was the thing I used to protect myself from people's curiosity. I'd grab on to it with both hands to stop them from ripping it off my face. They thought it was a chance to have some fun. One would prod me in the backside, and they would all burst into fits of raucous laughter. Sometimes, when I got really angry, I'd stay in the tea and coffee room. Baddah, the youngest, and the one who laughed loudest when they were having their fun, would come and put me right with a ten-riyal note, and I would go and serve them again, feeling broken, aggrieved, and totally alienated.

In the bus station waiting room a Bangladeshi cleaner in blue overalls asked him to lift his feet up. He lifted them up, feeling a momentary importance as the cleaner passed the cords of the mop under his feet to clean the tiles. He wanted to ask the man if he would quit his job if one of his superiors went too far insulting him, but he decided not to. He wondered if he had been a bit hasty not showing up for work for three consecutive days without offering any excuse or submitting his resignation, so he could receive his due rights. But what rights are they, Turad? Do you have any rights in this city? Who would look out for your rights? Weren't you just a monkey for those bastards to amuse themselves with when they had nothing better to do?

It was a bad day when I took tea in for Badr in his distinctive black mug. I never refused a request he made. He was the one who had intervened to get me my job back after I had fallen out with the director. In fact, no one in the ministry could turn down a request from him, because his father was the owner of the biggest supplier of office materials in the city. He secured all the ministry's needs in terms of office furniture and photocopying equipment in exchange for paying a considerable percentage of the purchase price to the director of financial affairs. How could the tarnished director refuse a request from Badr when Badr paid him many times more than his salary? Anyway, I went into their office, and no sooner had I put down the tea on rich boy Badr's desk than one of the damn employees jumped out at me with a screech and knocked me to the floor. Their laughter hit me in the head like bullets. One of them rushed over and tried to tear off the *shmagh* I'd wrapped tightly around my face. I wasn't ready to grab the *shmagh* because I was leaning on my hand to help myself stand up again, and all I felt was the *shmagh* come away in his blasted hand. Immediately I placed my hand over my ear, which made them think I was covering my ear because they were laughing so loudly. It never occurred to them that I didn't have a left ear. I stood up and rushed over to the guy who was waving my *shmagh* about in the air like an American cowboy, keeping my left hand over my left ear and trying to grab my *shmagh* with the right. I managed to catch the edge of the *shmagh* and pull it out of his grip, but he pulled it back suddenly, using both of his hands, and dragged me toward the edge of his desk. I put out both of my hands to avoid slamming my face into the desk but was unable to prevent my mouth from colliding with the wooden edge, and I tasted the blood as it stained my teeth. The secret of my left ear was out. One of them shouted, "Hey, guys, his ear's cut off!"

They roared with laughter, so much so that one of them collapsed across the top of the desk, while another, tears rolling down his cheeks, shouted, "It must be van Gogh. Hahahaha."

Their stupid laughter echoed around the room, and one of them asked, "Who's van George, then?"

"Hahaha, van Gogh, you idiot. He's the Dutchman who cut off his ear and gave it to his girlfriend." They couldn't control themselves. Even the green curtains that had been hanging there for years were shaking.

"Do you think Turad has a girlfriend?" one of them chimed in. "I bet he doesn't even take his *shmagh* off in bed. Hahaha."

Suddenly Turad saw a young woman struggling to pull a huge suitcase across the tiles of the waiting room. He jumped to his feet like a true Bedouin gentleman in order to lend her a hand. When his hand brushed against hers holding the handle of the suitcase, she glared at him coldly. "I wanted to help you," he said.

"Do you know me?" snapped the woman.

"No," he replied stupidly, "I don't know you, but..."

"Well, go help yourself, then," she interrupted, "before you help other people."

He withdrew, defeated, and noticed that the passengers scattered around the few seats in the waiting room were sizing him up, pondering his shabby clothes and the *shmagh* tied around his face as if it were part of his anatomy. That woman was the last thing he needed. "I won't go back to my seat," he whispered to himself. "I'll go straight to the ticket counter, and when the clerk asks me where I'm going, I'll tell him I'm going to Hell."

The Secret of
the Sad Singing

THE WAITING ROOM STARTED TO YIELD
to darkness and tranquillity, having rid itself of the
throng of passengers who had minutes before gathered
at the door of the bus, then boarded and departed. Still,
there were new passengers arriving through the main
entrance all the time, while others, who had taken their
places in the hall earlier on, had laid their heads on
their bags and were immersed in deep, dreamy sleep.

Turad stood in the middle of the waiting room,
slowly deciphering the names of the cities and the
numbers of the buses on the huge electronic signboard.
He could not find Hell among them. His breathing fal-
tered and his footsteps became heavy, as it occurred to
him that Hell accosted him on all sides and surrounded
him wherever he went: Is there a worse Hell than this,
Turad? Will you remain a fugitive wherever you are?
He turned his stooping frame to the seat where he had

been sitting but found an old man had taken his place. Next to him was a little girl cradling a bottle of Coca-Cola in her hand. She had taken off her shoes and socks and placed them on the table next to the glass of tea that Turad had left there moments before. As soon as the old man saw him, he shifted nervously in his seat as if to apologize. Turad motioned to him to stay where he was. He did not need to sit there. He picked up the glass of cold tea and was about to move away when the old man called to him. Turad turned to see the gentleman waving a green file, which he hadn't noticed when he had been sitting there a little while ago: "You've forgotten your file." Turad took it, concealing the unease that fluttered between his slightly bulging eyes, so as not to offend the old man by denying his connection to the file. He accepted it cautiously, as he had the abandoned glass of tea. The owner of the glass of tea must have been reading the file before they announced the departure of his bus, and he had hurried off to make sure he got a window seat, leaving the tea and forgetting the file. Turad thought to himself that it would help him pass the time on the long boring journey through the night.

Outside the bus station, on the sidewalk wet with drizzle, Turad stood and contemplated the dark sky, which seemed so close he reached out to touch its textured surface. When the sky comes that close to someone does it mean his end is near, and a cloud that looks like a riding camel will spirit him away? Suddenly two young men walked past him with their bags slung over their shoulders. They were laughing loudly, and he immediately turned toward them, but they walked on, paying him no attention. He placed the green file under his arm, and with his free hand checked that his *shmagh* was well wrapped around his face. He always felt extremely annoyed with anyone who laughed too loudly; it reminded him of the unbearable humiliation he had suffered at the hands of the young men at the ministry. Damn! What am I supposed to do about this missing ear? Wherever I go and however far I travel I will always meet people, and they will discover my secret even if I do keep this *shmagh* wrapped around my head.

A neon sign shining opposite the entrance to the station caught his attention. He crossed the road toward the small snack bar nestled under the flashing sign and ordered a chicken *shawerma* without pickles. As the Turkish *shawerma* man sharpened his long knife, Turad gazed at his clean, finely defined ear, which glowed red in the light and heat of the flames. The Turkish *shawerma* man swaggered proudly, showing off his beautiful ear as he carved tender slices from the huge cone-shaped column of chicken wrapped around the spit, piled them up with his spoon, added some fries, and spread a dollop of mayonnaise on the bread. His other ear glowed with every jolt of his body, thanks to the strong light of the halogen lamp that was positioned just above his head and the pile of chicken. And all the time the Turk was singing a sad song in a language Turad could not understand; he just kept staring at that captivating left ear as he wondered about the secret of the sad singing. How on earth could someone who possessed such a wonderfully perfect ear be sad? Wasn't it enough that he could walk down the street and hold his head up high, without having to hide his face in a *shmagh* or a *ghutra* or a *kufiyya*, and no one dare be sarcastic or make fun of him? True enough, his hair was thinning slightly around the temples, but baldness is a distinguishing feature of mature men. Men in their forties and even some in their thirties are prone to baldness, and women don't find anything wrong with that. But who in the world suffers from a missing ear except me? It's true that I explain to everyone who discovers the matter of this accursed ear that it's a deformity I've suffered since birth. It's true that some have consoled me with the fact that there are other people in the world with missing ears, either as a result of deformity from birth or war wounds. But what caused you to lose your ear, Turad? Aaah, if only you'd been in some courageous war and it had been blown off . . . not just your ear but your head, too.

Turad took the *shawerma*, wrapped in paper, and paid the Turk three one-riyal notes that had become covered in sweat as he held them in his palm. He stood on the sidewalk by the corner of the snack bar. There were no seats or tables inside or outside. The place was so small that there was room for only the *shawerma* grill and a small counter with trays containing scrambled egg, liver, kidney, and deep-fried falafel arranged in a row behind a glass screen. Flies roamed freely over the food, or landed audaciously on the Turk's shiny red ear, and he shooed them away every couple of moments with his bare arm while his hand gripped the sharp knife.

Turad unwrapped the paper from the top of the *shawerma* as a police car raced past with sirens wailing. Its grim blue light slapped the sides of the street, Turad's face, and the Turkish *shawerma* man's ear. Turad cursed as he bit into the *shawerma*: Who are the crazy bastards after now? Are they going to arrest a thief? Then what? Will they pluck his ear off like you pick a flower? Or will they chop off the hand he stole with? Or will they throw him in some cell where clean water, fresh air, and people will never reach him?

After two bites of the *shawerma*, Turad's thick mustache was covered in mayonnaise. He wiped it with the back of his hand, and his eyes followed the knife of the Turkish *shawerma* man as it whistled through the

air like the sword of a hardened and courageous warrior. It made him wonder whether he should grab the
knife and cut off the arrogant Turk's ear. But then, he
thought to himself, what would I do with it? Plant it
where my missing ear once was? Then I'd have two
ears, one dark and one red. Good Lord, son of Khazna!
Would that put an end to your tragedy? Of course it
wouldn't. It wouldn't change a thing. What would you
do with that red ear, then? I'd throw it to the dogs or
the wolves.

A black cat walked past, stopped, and meowed as it
rubbed its body against Turad's leg. He tore a piece of
chicken from the *shawerma*, as if he were ripping off the
Turk's ear, and threw it to the cat. It swallowed the
morsel and then walked around him again, meowing
continuously, until finally it sat in front of him on the
sidewalk, leaving him under no illusion that it would
stop staring at him as long as he was devouring the
shawerma. He threw it what was left in his hand and
walked off along the sidewalk, cursing all the cats in the
city. Does the damn thing want me to cut off my only
ear and throw that to it? He remembered the guys in the
ministry. They had likened him to a Dutch artist named
van Gogh who had cut off his ear and given it to the
woman he loved. And you, Turad, you dog, would willingly give your only ear to a stray black cat.

He darted out into the road without looking, and a speeding car almost ran him over. The brakes screeched, the horn blared, and the driver cursed and spat, but Turad didn't turn to look at him. He just hurried onto the sidewalk, the *shmagh* wrapped tightly around his face, gripping his old olive green overcoat and the green file. When he reached the other side of the road he noticed that the spray of rainwater thrown up by the car's tires had splashed the bottom of his *thobe*.

He turned into the bus station, shuffling along in his wet muddy shoes. But this time, instead of heading for the ticket counter or the signboard with the names of the towns and bus numbers, he found himself walking to the end of the waiting room near the toilets, where he sat down far from the other passengers and people waiting. He slouched in the seat and raised his head toward the ceiling. Having eaten, and feeling the warmth and security of the waiting room, he was overcome by a sudden drowsiness. Without straightening himself up he turned to one side and was shocked to see a huge mural that took up two-thirds of the wall. He tried to explore the details of the painting. At the bottom were thick undulating lines that looked like waves on the ocean, or sand dunes. Perhaps because the colors ranged from brown to light and dark yellow to orange, they resembled sand dunes more than anything else. In the center of the picture he could see abstract figures walking in a line that appeared to be a caravan of she-camels. Above them, an orange sun was setting. On the right side of the picture a man—whose features could not be clearly discerned—was walking and dragging a stick behind him as if he were drawing lines with it in the sand. To the far left were three dogs or wolves. They were more likely wolves, because their muzzles were raised toward the horizon.

As soon as Turad's eyes fell on what looked like wolves, he shut them tight. "Damn," he muttered, then thought to himself, Where did those wolves come from? What stupid artist painted this picture and put howling wolves in it? Could it be the one those fools in the ministry said looked like me, the Dutchman van Gogh? No way! Someone like him who lived in Holland would paint only trees and fields and flowers. He wouldn't have anything to do with deserts, camels, and wolves. I wonder if he really cut off his ear and gave it to his lover, gave it to a woman, a mere woman? God! Is there a woman anywhere who deserves one of us to cut off a body part and give it to her, especially an ear? You idiot, van Gogh! You cut off your beloved ear that allows you to hold your head high and not be ashamed. You willingly cut it off and sent it to a woman. You must be mad. True, I cut off my ear like you, or to be more precise I lost it one night, but not for a woman. Never! Even if I had three cars, not one, or even two like the rest of mankind, I would never offer one to a woman, whoever that woman was.

A woman bordering on plump emerged from the ladies' toilets nearby. As she walked past him the two eyes peering from behind her black veil cast him a glance. She looked like the woman he had tried to help earlier, before she had cursed him and chased him away. It was indeed the very same woman; he recognized the tender white hand that his own hand had grazed when he had tried to take the handle of her heavy suitcase. He watched her pass, but his mind was elsewhere as his eyes focused on her huge posterior. In fact, the face of Tawfiq the Slave had appeared to him, glistening with a flood of tears. It was the first time Turad had seen him cry as Tawfiq bemoaned the fate that had plucked him out of the Sudan and cast him forth upon the high seas for so many days that he thought he would never again set foot on dry land.

The first time I saw him was in the tea and coffee room at the ministry. At first I thought he was either an idiot or a mute, for he never answered anyone who spoke to him or joked with him. He simply responded to the demands of the staff and made the morning and afternoon tea. Even so, he showed me how to prepare coffee with cloves, and tea with mint, ginger, and cinnamon.

Then he taught me how to make the tea with sage that the director liked, and how to arrange the coffee and tea tray by placing, for example, the glass of tea on a small glass saucer with a lump of sugar and a small gold spoon on the edge; he showed me how to carry the tray in my left hand while my right hand lifted the glass and set it down on the table in the director's office; and he told me how to interpret the director's gestures and facial expressions when he was engrossed in conversation with his guests. Amm Tawfiq, as they called him, taught me the secrets of the trade. He even warned me not to fall into the trap of reacting to the sarcasm of the staff, or of getting worked up about their jokes and pranks, otherwise they'll enjoy making fun of you when they've nothing better to do. That's what he told me, but I didn't take his words seriously, and I became a plaything for the guys. In the end I was obliged to escape. Yes, it was escape and defeat.

Silence was Amm Tawfiq's approach, and there was wisdom in his silence. His face was stern, never laughing, not even smiling. I used to wonder if he could laugh or smile with anyone when he left the ministry building. Did he cry when he was alone? Did he carry a secret deep inside himself that he could not reveal to anybody? I asked myself these questions when I first got to know him. I used to watch his face as he prepared the coffee and tea. He had a plump, round face full of old pockmarks. But despite that he had two intact ears, broad and flat, that looked like the ears of an elephant. He took great pains to keep his beard clean, and every two days he removed any white hairs that had sprouted. The hairs in his mustache he left, although he trimmed it; his thick lips always seemed cracked and swollen. On his head he wore a white *ghutra* that had turned a miserable yellow, and underneath it a skullcap with gold guineas embroidered around the rim that covered the frizzy hair on his temples.

The Journey of
Eternal Torment

"SIXTY YEARS AGO, OR MORE, I WAS IN the village of Umm Hibab. I was eight years old at the time. The village was more or less in the center of the Sudan. There weren't many huts in it, and I lived in one of them with an old man and his wife. I had lost my mother after she ran away from her master, Ahmad al-Hajj Abu Bakr. One night the slave traders came and burned down all the huts. I managed to escape toward Shindi and Barbar in the north, but my uncle Fadlallah Adam, and his wife, Bakhita Uthman, were taken away. We were asleep when we heard the screaming. I jumped through the door and saw the hut of Idris al-Sayyid, the cripple, engulfed in flames. His wife, al-Sabr Zayn, was trying to drag him out. He was screaming at her. I didn't know if he was screaming from the fire that was burning his head and clothes, or because he wanted her to leave him to die. Before I disappeared into the jungle I saw al-Sabr Zayn running around her burning hut. She was like a human torch running around the hut screaming, after her hair had caught fire. Can you believe it, Turad, even now, after sixty years or more I can still hear her screams before I sleep?"

"So where did you escape to?" asked Turad.

Amm Tawfiq gestured to me to be patient, stood up, and moved sluggishly across the room to the stove. The tea had been boiling for a long time. He took off the wooden shelf two glasses with the Kraft cheese label still stuck on them, washed them, and poured tea into each one, taking care to lift the old brass teapot high into the air so that he could enjoy the steam rising from the stream of poured tea.

"I, my friend, I went into the jungle. I'd walk through the bush by night and sleep by day so I wouldn't fall into the hands of the slave traders. The country was awash with traders in human beings, and the tribes that dealt in slaves were everywhere: the Kababish in the region of al-Bitana, the Ta'ayasha in Kurdufan, the Ruzaiqat and Musairiya in Bahr al-Ghazal, and the Rashayda in Port Sudan and Sawaken. The slave traders were crawling over every inch of the Sudan. Anyway, after a few days I reached al-Hasahisa. I stayed there for more than a month. I got to know a lot of people, mostly runaways. Some were branded on their backs or necks. We were just like animals, living off grass and vermin. Hunger began to take its toll, until we fell into the trap."

"How?"

Amm Tawfiq stood up, walked two steps over to the window, and pulled it shut. "It's getting cold," he said. "Riyadh nights are terrible in November. Now, you were asking me about the trap. Listen, my friend, it was a pleasant time, I mean, the weather was mild, like the daytime now, and there was a lovely breeze. There we were, a bunch of people who couldn't find anything to eat, and suddenly the breeze carried to us a wonderful aroma, a sweet smell, the smell of delicious cooking. We stood up and set off in a long line toward the smell. The farther we walked the stronger the smell grew. It went up our nostrils and made us dizzy. We wound our way between the tree trunks, and if a clump of bushes or a thicket of trees got in our way, we didn't go around it for fear of losing the smell but rather climbed straight over it and trampled the thorns with our bare feet. Eventually, in the distance we saw a fire surrounded by small stones on every side. We couldn't see the spit because the smoke was too thick and the wind was blowing it in our direction. The smell was driving us wild. We were just about to rush toward the fire when one of the older and more mature members of the group signaled to us to stop. He said the fire might belong to the slave traders or some similar armed band. Someone else said, 'Why don't we send one of us to investigate. If they catch him that'll be only one and the rest of us can escape.' Everyone said to him, 'You go and have a look!' but he refused. Then we all agreed to pounce together. If we didn't find anybody we'd steal the food and run, and if the owners of the food attacked us we'd stand and fight together. So we charged all at once and ran up to the fire where the skewers were grilling, and stopped. There was no one there. Then just as we were about to grab the food, we were surrounded by masked men. Some were carrying rifles; others had chains and ropes over their shoulders. One from our group, a young man named Bakhit, launched himself at two of their men. He was well built and powerful, and he sent them flying, but before he could reach the trees one of them picked up his rifle and took aim. A bullet whistled through the air and thudded into Bakhit's back. He fell onto his face and lay there silent as a stone. We all stood where we were, unable to utter a word. Some fell to their knees in fear. The men carrying the ropes rushed forward and began to tie our hands, while those carrying rifles continued to point them at us. Imagine what they were cooking? The bastards had put lumps of fat on the skewers and placed them on the fire. See how they tricked us, Turad? With fat and gristle roasting on the fire. They couldn't even be bothered to trick us with real meat."

"But you saw the fat," interrupted Turad. "So why did you run up to the fire?"

"No, we didn't. We didn't see a thing. There was lots of smoke. It was everywhere. No one could see anything. Anyway, one of the men uncovered his face, and he looked like he was from the Ja'aly tribe. His eyes were yellow and his nose a little flat. Next to him walked a strange-looking man who I learned later was a Bedouin from Arabia. They inspected us very carefully, with the Ja'aly paying particular attention as he looked us up and down, and walked around the women to examine them from front and behind. Then he started to divide us into groups. I was a boy, slim and good-looking, and he put me with three other boys whose facial hair still hadn't sprouted. He pointed to us, and I heard him say, 'Those are fivers.'"

"What's a fiver?" asked Turad.

"If you measure him from his ankle to his earlobe he's five spans."

Automatically Turad felt for his left ear. Amm Tawfiq noticed him. "If he has an ear missing," he said, "they measure him on the other side." They both had a good laugh.

"By the way, you must tell me the story of your ear when I've finished. Right then, when they had divided us up into groups, they tied each group together and drove us along in front of them. Two Ja'alys walked in front as guides, and behind the Bedouin strangers were more Ja'alys, and on all sides we were surrounded by men with rifles. Those strangers were being protected by the Ja'aly tribe from attacks by bands of thieves until they arrived safely back at their ship. They took us for miles through forest and jungle, down into valleys, and up over highlands, and whenever we stumbled or fell they'd kick us or whip us with a switch of plaited leather. We walked eastward for days on end, until finally we climbed up into some mountains. They took us into a cave through a dark narrow entrance, but once we were inside it opened up. It was their secret hideout, and there they gathered around thirty slaves."

"Why didn't you escape?" asked Turad, urging him on. Tawfiq poured some tea, which appeared to have gone cold from the sound it made and the froth that formed at the rim of the glass.

"Before I was caught I had heard about the son of Halima from al-Qatina. The slave traders had taken him to al-Fasher. He managed to get away without them noticing and escaped to the police station at Umm Kidada. They returned him to his mother. But the men who captured him were only a small band, and they weren't armed or well organized. I mean, it wasn't a proper expedition. And I've just told you how Bakhit was killed when he tried to run away."

Turad nodded his head in agreement and sipped his tea with a grave expression in his eyes as he took the left-hand side of his *ghutra* and threw it over his right shoulder.

"Anyway, the next day they took us to Shindi, and by the time we reached Barbar our number had dwindled. Two of us dropped dead on the way. I don't know where the others disappeared to. They might have sold them at the Shindi market to recoup the cost of the expedition, and so they could pay the Ja'alys who had protected them as they moved through the country. We left Barbar with a huge herd of sheep and headed for Sawaken on the coast. They put us on a medium-sized boat with sacks of corn and sealed chests in the cargo hold down below. It was almost pitch-black. They herded the sheep from Barbar onto the deck. The boat pulled away from the port of Sawaken, and we set sail. It was *hajj* season, about a month and a half before the *hajj* itself. We spent long days and nights at sea. Some nights we would hear muffled noises in the distance. It was the sound of the foreign patrol boats as they shined their prying spotlights onto passing boats. They were observing ships and steamers on the Red Sea. But as soon as the white man approached with his shining torches to inspect the boat's cargo, the smell of animal dung from the deck would overwhelm him. He'd pull back, give the crew the thumbs up, and our boat would continue on its way.

"During the Red Sea days some of the sailors hung yellow flags over the railings above the cabin. The skipper would say a word to one of the guys, and he would take the flag, shimmy up the mast, and unfurl it. We then realized it was a really huge banner, which could be seen from miles away. The boy would tie it firmly to the mast, then attach it with ropes to the prow. The banner would billow and thrash in the wind and make a noise like the sound of a whip lashing a slave's back. That yellow sign would make the foreign patrol boats avoid the boat and not stop it for inspection, for in seafaring terms the yellow flag means the boat is infested with the plague.

"After we had spent days in the pen below deck, four men came down the steps to us. One of them was a black man, Eritrean I think. They handed us *ihram* clothes for the *hajj*. They had been used before, and they were dirty. I did not know how to put the wrap around my waist. The Eritrean took me into the toilet. I almost tripped over the piles of ropes and hooks as he dragged me by the wrist, and I held the *ihram* in my other hand. He was cursing me in a language I couldn't understand, and his face was dark and angry. Before he tied the wrap he began to fiddle with my ass with his huge hand, then he grabbed the back of my neck and pushed me over, and that's when I felt his cock like a *hashaab*. Do you know what a *hashaab* is?"

Turad shook his head from side to side as if he didn't understand anything of Tawfiq's difficult dialect.

"Not to worry," Tawfiq went on. "A *hashaab* is a rock-hard plant. We used to extract gum from it in Kusti and al-Qadarif. Anyway, I couldn't scream or cry. All I did was clean myself up after he'd finished. I tied the wrap around my waist and went out after him into the cargo hold. He rushed up the stairs onto the deck, and I never set eyes on him again."

Official Documents

AFTER TURAD HAD CONTEMPLATED THE names of the towns displayed on the screen, he realized that towns were no different from anything else he had known in his life. They were just towns, one very much like the next, with nothing to distinguish it from the others; like the faces of the teachers at the night school where he had learned to read and write; like the shapes of the cars he used to wash, all set out in lines in the ministry parking lot; like the redundant faces of the ministry staff, from the minister to the archive clerk; like women's black *abbayas*; like streets; like the ornate china coffee cups on the shelf in the tea and coffee room; like everything in this country.

He turned his weary body, leaving the screen behind him, but then looked around again at the first city at the top of the list and said to himself, I'll go to Arar. Surely it can't be much different from Hell. The best thing about it is that it's right on the border of Hell, one step and I'll be in another country. I'm not looking for Heaven, or Paradise, or even an easy life. All I want is a place where people will respect me, not abuse me or treat me like a dog. I ran away from my own folk because of the tribe. I ran away from the palace, and from the parking lot, and from the ministry, and now at last I'm trying to run away from Hell. He said this, then walked toward the ticket counter, praying to Allah as he did so to spare himself the evil of eternal Hell, and to limit his torment to just this one Hell he was living in now.

"One way to Arar, please."

He took the ticket and placed it carefully in his top pocket, and gripping the green file under his armpit, he made for the seats at the far end of the waiting room. He selected an isolated chair, with the window behind it looking out onto the street, sat down, and put the green file on his lap. He ensured his *shmagh* was well wrapped, opened the file from the right, and began to read:

INCIDENT REPORT

Today, Friday the 13th of Muharram 1398 AH, at exactly four a.m., a newborn baby was discovered near the mosque of Abdullah Ibn al-Zubair in the al-Sadd al-Gharbi district. The baby has a mutilated face; one of its eyes has been removed. It had been

placed in a banana crate and was wrapped in a
white cotton sheet. The discovery was made by Mr.
Muhammad al-Daw, who described how he found the
baby lying among its afterbirth in the crate. He took
the baby to his home nearby, where he cleaned it,
cut the umbilical cord, and then informed the police.
May Allah bear witness to what we have said herein.

Signatures of witnesses

Turad looked carefully at the name of the police
department, and at the emblem and branch name at the
top right-hand side of the paper. He tried to decipher
the spidery handwritten signatures of the witnesses.
He then turned over the page, read the title, and moved
down the page:

MEDICAL REPORT

Symptoms: The baby's left hip is dislocated. In
addition, severe damage suffered to the tissue
surrounding the right eye socket as a result of the
traumatic loss of the eye. The baby is also suffering
from hepatitis and dehydration.

Treatment: The case needs to be kept in the hospital
for ten days and followed up six months after
discharge.

Medical Center Specialist   Duty Manager

Turad turned the page slowly but did not notice
the baby's name. He was too busy looking at the sen-
tence "severe damage suffered to the tissue surrounding

the right eye socket as a result of the traumatic loss of the eye."

Dear God, Turad thought to himself, how could a newborn baby lose its eye? There is no power and strength but in Allah. Why wasn't he in a cradle with his mother rocking him, singing him lullabies until he fell asleep? His bed was a banana crate, his room a street next to the Ibn al-Zubair mosque. His name is . . . he has no name, no date of birth, no mother and father, no brothers and sisters, no family, no home, no country. Damn this godforsaken country. This baby has grown up in Hell like me. He's living with us, Tawfiq and me, right now with this uncertainty. Turad went back to the first page and looked for the date of birth. He thought for a moment—he'd be about twenty—then thought, You've still got a long way to go before you're finished, you poor bastard, before you die and leave behind this insufferable Hell.

He turned the pages. One caught his eye, and he looked at it closely:

NAMING RECORD

Upon consulting the list of official names for new-born males and the list of names for mothers—both the original in our possession and the copy held at the hospital of the medical complex—the name selected for the newborn male is Nasir Abdulilah Hasan Abdullah. The name selected from the list of

mothers' names is Salha Abdulrahman Ahmad. It has
therefore been decided to name the newborn male,
file no: 921/1398, as above, Nasir Abdulilah Hasan
Abdullah, and to name his mother Salha Abdulrahman Ahmad.

Register signed by . . .

Can you imagine having a completely made-up
name? That chance alone had wished your name to be
Turad and not Matrud or Mas'ud because that's where
they stopped on the official list of names and gave you
an arbitrary name? Imagine that your father and grand-
father and mother all had made-up names, that you
were given a made-up life, like a hero in a film or
novel. The name is nothing like people's real names in
this infernal city. It stretches out like a wild endless
track, like a dark corridor in which you can't see anything, not even your hand. There's no goddamn definite article at the end, not like the well-known families
in our country. You are a nonentity, undefined, with
no known father or mother. How can you be made
definite, Nasir, if you are indefinite? True, my name is
Turad, Hunter, even though I am the one who is
hunted. And true, my name ends with the name of a
famous tribe from the desert heartland of Najd, and
true, I was a professional highwayman before my left
ear was ripped off. I wish my health would help me
now to steal and rob in the vast wilderness in broad

daylight, not like they do here, in the dark, between office walls and behind closed doors. But I am like you in every respect. We are both lost in this strange and unfamiliar city.

What I'm saying to you, young Nasir, is that I'd rather have a thousand definite articles chopped off my name. I'd rather have this whole tribe's name cut off and thrown into Hell than to have lost my ear. Do you know the most unpleasant feeling is sensing the person sitting next to me staring stupidly at my ear if I forget to cover it with the edge of my *shmagh*? Bastards! That's my missing ear. There, take it and piss on it! Just go to Hell and leave me alone.

The science teacher at the Ihsan Night School told us that hearing is the first sense that links the newborn baby to the world. In my case it was the one sense that cast me out from the world. For it I lost my health and vigor, my self-confidence, my family, my clan, and my job—everything. I wouldn't be exaggerating if I said it'd lost me my life. I don't remember the first thing I heard in my earliest days, but it wouldn't be anything other than the voice of my mother, the sheep bleating as they returned at sunset, or the running wind as it blew up the sand and beat against our tent.

The difference between us, Nasir, is that you lost your eye because of your ear, and I lost my ear because of my eye. My eye watered one still desert night, and my ear was whisked away, hot on the heels of that tear. As for you, your eye was snatched thanks to that infernal sense of hearing. If only your mother, Salha (as they named her), hadn't led astray your father, Abdulilah (the name they invented), and he hadn't succumbed to her soft, honeyed voice on the phone, then slept with her until you were conceived. You found yourself thrown just before dawn in a banana crate by the Ibn al-Zubair mosque, where you lost your right eye; maybe a dog or a hungry stray cat gnawed at it in the city night. All you could do was scream and cry just as I, one savage night in the desert, could do nothing but weep as my left ear was snatched away for a tear. Ah, Ya Turad, if only you'd held back that tear, your ear would still be in its place.

ANNOUNCEMENT OF BIRTH

Name of child: Nasir
Sex: male **Dead/alive:** alive
Place of birth: General Medical Complex
Date of birth AH: 1/7/1398
Date of birth AD: . . .
Time of birth: . . .
Name of father: Abdulilah Hasan Abdullah
   Nationality: Saudi
   Religion: Muslim
   Profession: Civil servant
Name of mother: Salha Abdulrahman Ahmad
   Nationality: Saudi
   Religion: Muslim

Just look at that for a coincidence! You've got only one eye and me one ear. You don't know your mother or father, and I don't know any other country than this Hell. The difference is that I hide the stump of my deformed ear with my *ghutra* or *shmagh*, whereas I imagine it would be quite difficult for you to hide your missing eye, Nasir. There's someone conspiring against us, Nasir, until the Day of Judgment. They stole your eye so you couldn't see, and now you spend your whole life asking and thinking about nothing except how you're going to hide it from people. They severed my ear so I can't hear, and I spend my life humiliated and insulted, concealing the shame of my injury.

Don't worry about it, my friend. If I saw you I'd suggest the perfect solution. Wear sunglasses. That way no one would see your eye. Always keep them on, even when you go to sleep. You see the world black when you're awake; why shouldn't you see black dreams when you're asleep?

If I saw you, Nasir without the definite article, unacknowledged nonentity, I'd tell you the stories of Tawfiq the Slave, who knew his mother but wasn't sure who his father was. He says lots of people bought his mother from the slave market, and most of them slept with her, though he doesn't know which one's vicious sperm grabbed his mother's egg. Was it her master, Ahmad al-Hajj Abu Bakr, whom she ran away from in the end, or was it one of the slave traders? Was it a trader in the slave market, or another of her owners?

If you only knew what Tawfiq the Slave lost. You and I, an eye and an ear, but him . . .

Turad laughed audibly, and one of the travelers sitting nearby shot him a worried and suspicious glance. Turad fell silent, and his thoughts scattered as he tried to look sane. It would be easy enough for them to pick him up and throw him into a mental institution. No one would ask after him. No one had asked after him for years. He had turned into a solitary desert plant, struggling against wind and drought and desolation. He wasn't even worth as much as a little *shafallah* bush, which could at least offer a lost camel the chance to exercise its teeth, or aid a Bedouin on a bitter night with fuel for a fire to warm his body. He was no longer any use to man nor beast except as an object of ridicule. He thought about working as a public or private clown. To be in a public place teasing a laugh out of women and children would be contrary to his Bedouin code. But to be a private clown in a palace would earn him plenty of money, which he could spend curing the nervous breakdown he was going to have. He wondered how he would be able to do something like that after he had spent so many years keeping his missing ear a secret. He had concealed it from curious eyes with his *shmagh* or *ghutra* while he worked at the ministry. Sometimes he wore the winter hat with the woolen ear pieces, even on blazing hot summer days, when he worked as a gate guard at the huge palace.

A Long Fight

MY MOTHER, KHAZNA, USED TO PAY MORE attention to me than to my two brothers. They considered me a courageous warrior, afraid of nothing. I loved the desert night and befriended the wolves. I would walk the crest of the dune while the wolf trotted along some distance away, keeping a wolfish eye on me but not thinking to attack. I would clock him with my wolf eye and not think to kill or harm him. I did not possess a weapon. I never liked carrying one. My weapons in those days were a courageous heart, sharp eyes like a hawk measuring up his prey, and my bare hands; with them I would bring down the animals I hunted or stole in the night. Why did I steal at night? Was it because I was afraid of horsemen, travelers, and caravans? Not at all. But I did not want to have to kill someone to defend myself, my plunder, or my property. For, yes, those things belonged to me. I had earned them with my wit, intelligence, and courage. I had outsmarted those who owned but didn't deserve them.

When I was a child I used to hunt wild rabbits, and occasionally catch the odd animal. I'd tear it limb from limb like the wolf does, light a fire in the pitch-black night, and grill enough to eat my fill. As I ripped the flesh with my sharp incisors, I'd see a she-wolf in the distance leading her youngsters, passing back and forth, observing me without approaching. When I finished my supper, I'd get up and be on my way. Without looking I'd sense the she-wolf hurrying to the spot where I had sat, then howling, her four little ones behind her.

My mother, Khazna, would miss me for a day or two, but as soon as she saw me she'd scold me for staying on my own in the desert. Then she'd tell me off for not bringing them anything I'd picked up in the wilderness. My father was well advanced in his years, and his eyesight was weak. There was only my brother Sayyaf left, after we lost my elder brother, Sayf. He had been abducted by a genie with long hair and deep dark eyes. They say he went out one night to relieve himself, when the genie fell in love with him and carried him off on her wings. Some said that my brother Sayf had become an inhabitant of the underworld. They even went as far as to say that he had become a great king in one of the genie kingdoms. Ah, my brother, won't you send me a woman from the genie tribes, or from the daughters of your royal guard? Send me a woman who will fall madly in love with me and whisk me away from this Hell to the regions of the netherworld. You might not be able to hear me, brother, but I swear to you that I sit alone in the desert late at night, relieving myself more than once, looking for a genie to love me and fly me away, but I see only wolves watching over me from afar; they are wary of me.

One night, as I was squatting down to relieve myself, the branches of a nearby acacia tree moved in the wind. It gave me a fright, and, terrified, I jumped to my feet. Can you believe it? I, who dreads neither death nor man, my hair stood on end, and my bowels churned. I immediately felt that it was not an acacia tree, nor a woman with long hair, deep dark eyes, and blushing cheeks. Not at all. The acacia branches were like an old genie hag glaring furiously at me, a human being who had woken her by urinating on her legs.

When I grew older I realized that my brother Sayf hadn't really been abducted by a genie. She was in fact a very beautiful woman. We called her Dabbaha, the Slaughteress, because whomever she glanced at would lose his mind and become hopelessly smitten with her. She was a daughter of the gypsies who used to pass through the Bedouin encampments. They would patch our tents and clothes, polish our coffeepots, mend our teapots, and sell pillows, rugs, and such wares. After

Sayf slept on a pillow of colored wool that one of their women had woven, he fell sick for three days. On the fourth day we couldn't find him or the pillow. My father waited for months; his eyesight weakened, but Sayf did not return.

One summer night I lay resting under an *awshaz* tree. I had grown tired of waiting for a caravan of travelers or pilgrims to pass. But then, after three nights of lying in wait, I spied a man in the distance leading a young russet camel, followed by three sheep. I lay down low—my chin scraping the ground—like a wild beast that has sighted its prey. I wanted to crawl to a spot where I could ambush him as he passed. I paused when I saw him turn with the camel toward the *awshaz*. As soon as he had gone a few steps beyond my hiding place, I rose to my feet, crept silently behind him, then pounced and threw my arms around his neck in an effort to bring him to the ground. He grabbed my wrists with his hands and threw me over his back. I rolled onto the sand in front of him and sprang to my feet in an attacking posture. The man wielded his club of knotted wood that looked like a serpent and was as long as a spear, and brandished it in my face. He demanded I move out of his way or he'd smash my skull. I refused and ordered him to hand over the camel and the sheep. He aimed a swift blow at my head, but I ducked just in time to hear the club whiz through the air, inches above me. Once again he raised the club in the air and brought it down with all his might toward my head. I grabbed it; he struggled to pull it from my hands, and I fought to extricate it from his, but he was strong and hardy. He tried to thrust it into my chest, and I did the same. He turned the club toward the ground; I resisted by lifting it up again. I kicked him suddenly in the hamstring, and he fell, with me on top of him, and his long club went flying. He managed to knock me off of him with his strong legs. I scrambled to my feet and threw my arms around him again in an effort to throw him, but his legs were well positioned, and his feet were planted firmly in the sand. I tried once more to get my arms around his neck, but he released my hands with remarkable strength. He was an excellent fighter. I had never met anyone so strong and powerful, and although our battle lasted nearly two hours, he never tired or waned. I felt my own strength sapped and believed he was stronger. I couldn't see his face well in the darkness, but his shining eyes seemed like the eyes of a hyena. His hair was long and tied back. His mustache hadn't been trimmed for so long that his mouth looked like the muzzle of a lynx. After our long contest, and during a moment of disengagement, I asked that we rest awhile. He agreed.

"Will you make peace?" I said.

"I will make peace," he said. "May Allah protect

you." As I placed my hand in his, I asked him if he would trust a highwayman. He laughed as he panted for breath: "I am a highwayman, too. This camel and these sheep are my takings today." He embraced me and said, "From today you will be my brother." He also said that he had never clashed with someone as strong and powerful as I was. Together we would be invincible. We would take lots of plunder. That night he honored me like an old friend. He slaughtered one of his sheep, and we made a fire of *ghada* wood after he had lit it with a little of the kindling that had been on the russet camel's back. He told me his name was Nahar, Daytime. I recall how he laughed when I said that Daytime stole and held people up only at night.

Nahar and I spent each day together. He kept me company, and I was good company for him. We said good-bye to the company of the wolves, and they no longer kept watch on us from afar. Indeed, as soon as they saw us they would hurry away; we no longer left them anything to eat. After Nahar and I divided our earnings, I would take my share to my mother, brother, and father.

Once I returned with Nahar from a long trip through the wadis and ravines to find my mother, Khazna, wailing and beating her breast, pulling out her white hair and tearing the front of her garment. As soon as she saw me approaching, driving a young fair-haired she-camel through the darkness, she ran toward me, hugged me, and wept. She told me my brother Sayyaf had carried my father off in the night in a woolen saddlebag and left him in the mountains for the wolves and the wild animals.

It was not an easy thing for him to do, carry off his father and leave him for the beasts to tear apart his body. The poor man was unable to defend himself or ward off the beasts because he was ailing, and his sight was weak. Sayyaf said my mother was a crazy old woman. He changed her name sarcastically from Khazna to Kharifa, which means "senile," for now she had reached her autumn years. My father, Sayyaf told me, went out one night, when grief and distress got the better of him, to look for my brother Sayf. He said he would find him and bring him back, whether he was with the genies as a king in their kingdom, or had been bewitched by a woman with long hair and deep dark eyes. Sayyaf heard him at the end of the night saying to himself, "I'll cut off her hair and weave it into shackles to bind that crazy bastard Sayf before I tie him to the back of my old camel."

At that point Turad was not convinced by his brother Sayyaf's account, nor was he able to trust the words of his mother, Khazna. Sayyaf may well have done it, for he was well-known for his violent moods and impetuousness. He had felt ignored and neglected after his brother Sayf became his parents' obsession day and night. Sayf's name was forever on their lips. If they were struck by famine, or there wasn't enough food, or if they were attacked, they would weep with anxiety, "Where are you, Sayf?" At the same time, they placed hope in Turad to help them survive, for he was known for his courage, generosity, and strength, even if he was a highwayman.

The old Bedouin woman Khazna continued to store in her head the secrets of the wilderness and the tribes. She mourned her firstborn, who had been stolen from her by a genie and enthroned as king of the underworld. She grieved for her husband, against whom her second son had conspired and fed to the wild beasts of the desert. And she wept for her youngest, who insisted on attacking caravans and travelers passing through the desert, stealing their goods and enjoying himself with his best friend, Nahar, before returning to the old woman who waited for him, her feeble frame all eaten away, on top of the little hill, as if she were a mother wolf brought out by hunger, or a mother camel crying inconsolably as she gazes into the horizon in search of her young one who has strayed or been taken by thieves.

She wouldn't stop digging in the sand. For nights on end she scooped and raked with her fingers, howling and snarling in anger, as she scraped away the sand in search of Sayf, who had descended to a kingdom beneath the ground. She dug also in the hope that she might find the bones of the father, her husband, whom the birds of prey and wild beasts of the desert had swooped down upon. From the first light of dawn on the first day she had been digging without respite. Every time her cracked fingers felt the branch of a *ghada* bush or the root of an *arta* bush buried in the sand, she would say to herself, "This is your leg bone, Abu Sayf." But as soon as she pulled up the root or the branch she would be consumed with grief and despair and would not utter a single word.

The worst time she lost her head, she'd been digging for two full nights when finally she unearthed the crumbling leg bone of some animal hunted many years ago by wolves, its broken skeleton buried in the sand. She picked up the bone and ran around looking for Turad. Around and around she ran, wailing as she gripped in her hand the evidence of Sayyaf's wicked deed. She ran in every direction until she collapsed from exhaustion, and then somehow managed to struggle to her feet and set off once again.

A Body Like
Ripe Fruit

ALL HE HAD WAS THE '76 TOYOTA CRES-
sida, in which he cruised the well-lit tree-lined streets. It
had been white before he painted it yellow and fixed the
taxi sign on the roof. He frequented all the markets
and malls and the terminals at the old airport, ferrying
strangers, women and children and young men, all day
long, from early morning until midnight. On weekends
his wanderings extended to the first threads of dawn.

With its round, pointed headlights, his car looked
like a bat as it peered down old alleyways, feeling its
way, bumping into walls. He loved his car. He looked
after it and decorated it and felt great sympathy for it.
On the back ledge he had put two cushions embroidered with tiny round mirrors like little moons that
scattered the blazing midday sun in all directions. Over
the dashboard he had arranged a piece of olive green
cloth from which dangled tassels of the same color.

From the rearview mirror hung a ping-pong ball covered in colored sequins, attached to one another by pins, so that they shimmered and glistened every time the Cressida rocked or jolted. On the inside of the driver's door he had put a picture of the actress Suad Hosni in a seductive pose, with pouting lips and her hair disheveled like a horse's tail, as she teased her fingers through it and looked provocatively at the camera. Every time he looked at her while waiting for a passenger or someone crossing the road, he felt like she was staring at him, and he would let out a long sigh and silently watch the women walking up and down the street.

Lots of women used him. He would drop them off all over the crowded city, taking short cuts through narrow alleyways and dingy back streets. He never gave any of them a single thought, although the smell of the perfume some of them wore made his head spin. Some of them would flirt with him or make suggestive or provocative gestures, but he always made up his mind that it was money he was after, not self-destruction.

Then one hot and clammy summer afternoon, as he was waiting in his yellow Cressida in a line of taxis opposite the law court in the town center, a woman got in the backseat before he had reached the front of the line; there were still three cabs in front of him. He turned to her: "It's not my turn yet, Missus."

And in a thin and very delicate voice she snapped: "I am not a Missus. And anyway, I'm in now, and I am not getting out again."

"That's not what I meant," he said with some embarrassment. "It's just that I can't pull away until these three in front of me pull away first." To the right was the sidewalk and to the left a barrier. He pointed to them as he explained to her, but she interrupted him, her voice like drops of soft rain taking him completely by surprise: "Not to worry. I'll wait with you." Then she rolled the window halfway down and huffed in displeasure at the relentless onslaught of the heat. As he pulled the car away from the busy commercial center, she told him where she was going. A number of questions crowded into his head, and the sequin-covered ping-pong ball began to sway violently: Why did she bypass the first three cars and choose mine, even though one of those in front was a new Caprice, and much more luxurious than my cheap thing? The AC alone is worth a whole other car in the kind of scorchers we have in this country.

She interrupted his thoughts as she moved along the backseat and sat directly behind him.

"Uffff," she went, "by God, it's hot!" Then she asked him to take a less congested route. He turned up a side road in one of the new districts and headed west; the yellow light of the sun poured down onto the front windshield. Suddenly he felt a movement behind him, which was compounded by the pressure of her knee in the back of his seat. He looked in the mirror and noticed her carefully penciled eyes; she had pulled aside the black veil from her face and was using a tissue to wipe off the drops of sweat that had gathered on her forehead. She looked at his eyes in the mirror and did not once avert her gaze. She asked him his name and about his work and other quick things, and he answered as if he were drugged or bewitched. Before she got out of the car she gave him a fifty-riyal note with a white, tender-skinned hand, but he protested and swore he would not take anything from her. She insisted, and when he refused, she tossed the note onto the seat beside him and walked away.

He watched her as she made her way toward the gate of the house—not a traditional or mud house, but a modern house, with the blazing flowers of a bougain-villea hanging luxuriantly over the wall. She was tall and slim, and as she lifted her *abbaya* to her waist, a yellow skirt with black and honey-colored flowers showed beneath it. As she closed the gate she looked back toward him. She had taken off her head covering, and she shook her jet-black hair from side to side like a frisky mare. He smiled and sighed before shifting into first and slowly pulling away. He contemplated the house and its two front windows and the trees, and the electricity cables that ran along the wall. The instant he turned onto the main street he stretched out his hand to the passenger seat to feel for the fifty-riyal note. He put it to his nose to smell it, and as he did so a piece of paper fell into his lap. It bore the name of a clothing shop, and when he turned it over he was shocked to find a telephone number and, written underneath it, "12 might." At first he read it as "might," but then said to himself, Maybe it's "midnight" but she didn't bother to write the word out in full. There wasn't a telephone line in the modest apartment he shared with a colleague from work. Where would he find a telephone after midnight? He decided to visit an old friend who had an apartment in the town center with a telephone. At night her voice was softer, warmer, and more affectionate. She was young and divorced and lived with her elderly parents; her father was an invalid, and she looked after him. She said she had fallen in love with him the moment she had seen him. She spoke of many things:

I didn't finish my shopping that day. I was rushing to a clothes shop. I wanted to return a baggy red blouse that was the wrong size. I was intending to take it back before the sunset prayer call, before the shops closed, but as I was passing the taxi rank I noticed you playing with your mustache

and I felt something inside, something electric, and
after I had gone a few steps past your car I
turned around and got in. You might say I'm a
bit forward, but honestly it's the first time that's
ever happened. Something made me turn around.
I couldn't control myself.

She spoke hot, stormy, nocturnal words, and he
was drawn along, oblivious to everything around him.
He moved into his friend's flat and started to stay up
until dawn. He loved her intensely, and she fell madly
in love with him. He didn't bother with his car anymore, and he didn't decorate it. He started, instead, to
care for his face, look after his clothes, and stay up until
dawn listening to her soft voice, which soothed his
loneliness and the gloomy melancholy of night. The first
time he met her after making arrangements by phone,
she got into the taxi in front of al-Farazdaq Bookshop
on the main street near her house, and took her place
in the backseat as if she were with a driver. After he
had gone a little way down the main road, she asked
him to turn into a side street, and she hadn't been in his
little car for long before she signaled to him to stop. He
stopped. She stepped out, and as she got in next to him
she held out her pale, delicate hand to shake his. Her
hand was immersed in the vastness of his own. He
concealed his bewilderment by asking her how on earth

he was supposed to drive around the streets with her next to him. "I am your wife," she told him. "Should a taxi driver's wife sit in the backseat like a foreign woman?" He liked her words, her logic, and the supple fullness of her hand as it lay gently in his. Then her slender fingers with the red-painted nails intertwined with his. And, as if to remember forever the empty side street, and the houses that stood down one side and the school wall that stood on the other, he lifted her hand to his lips and kissed it.

He thought of the song "Wounded Heart" by Muhammad Abdu as she offered him his first kiss. After that he felt the town was different. He started to notice lots of things as he drove around. He noticed the girls in the streets, looked up at the trees, contemplated the neon signs, and he'd share a joke with the shopkeepers, read the papers, and buy magazines. He looked for books of folk poetry, and he listened to the latest songs and took in the words rather than just humming along to the tune as he had done before.

They drowned together in a bottomless sea of passion, and wandered down roads and streets and alleys. She kept on her black scarf and veil in the public thoroughfares and took them off whenever they sneaked, like two thieves of the night, into a side alley so she could steal a kiss from him. When she tried to do it on a main road that was full of shops, under the pretext that it was empty and the middle of the night, he had refused out of caution, even though her left hand insisted on going to its usual place.

Her body was clamoring now and had ripened like a piece of fruit. She led him one night to a deserted place on the outskirts of town. He pulled the taxi up to the end of a quiet, dusty lane in one of the newer quarters and turned the lights off, and she suddenly turned toward him. She wrapped her arms around him, then pulled him toward her in her seat and made him taste the full measure of her sadness, loneliness, and crushing isolation. He was like a young, wild animal that doesn't know the way through the gates of the forest. He felt her tentatively, curiously, full of desire, and she showed him the way, patient and tender, leading him by the hand like one would do for another who does not know, helping him until he understood his goal, and reached full pleasure. "You will marry me," she told him. "I will marry you," he said. He loved her so much, and she was addicted to his love. They enjoyed the pleasure many times, until one day she wept with him like a little bird at the slaughter. "The fruit of our love is growing in my womb," she told him. He was perturbed and promised her they would resolve the matter as soon as possible. After he had explained to his family his desire to marry, he mentioned her family's name. They laughed for a long time. His mother assured him she would look for a suitable bride, but he objected. "You are a son of the tribe," they told him. "You are a purebred, a son of free men. How can you marry a woman with no origin or breeding?" And when they noticed his insistence, his brother threatened to kill him, and waved the shotgun in his face, "Don't even think about it. Don't even think about that common woman."

The invalid father did not notice the swollen belly, and the mother, with her fading sight, did not or could not make out the growing womb sheltered beneath the wide housedresses. The fetus played lightheartedly while the woman's heart fluttered with terror. She spent the whole night waiting for the accursed telephone, which maintained a perpetual silence. She tried to find a way to contact him so he could help her out of this dilemma, so that together they could bury this secret forever, but he had left nothing. There was no trace of him. She wept the whole night long, cursing the telephone, tribes, and taxis; the streets, lust, and love; the *souk*, the shops, and the baggy red blouse; she cursed "Wounded Heart," all songs and folk poems.

After her belly had grown even rounder she decided to phone a childhood friend from primary and middle school days, and together look for an urgent solution to this scandalous predicament, even if it would mean her demise and her parents left with no one to support them. How many times she thought of crossing the highway so a speeding car could run her down; it wouldn't even matter if it were a taxi with a ping-pong ball covered in brightly colored sequins dangling from the rearview mirror. "Anything to put an end to this interminable nightmare."

She went with her friend, as the contractions started, to an old woman in al-Adul, a poor, working-class district. The old woman's driver, her partner in those operations, picked them up in a neutral place they had described to him over the phone. After she had given birth to a little boy with olive skin, the old woman placed him with his afterbirth and accompanying blood in a banana crate, prepared for that purpose, lined with a torn plastic bag. The driver covered the crate with an ample piece of cloth and casually carried it away. Off he went, after midnight, winding his way through streets and alleys until he entered al-Sadd al-Gharbi neighborhood, drove past the laundry with its neon sign switched off, the central stores, and into the square in front of the Ibn al-Zubair mosque. There he stopped the white sedan in the still night and got out, peering furtively as he did so down the alleys that led onto the square. He opened the backdoor and lifted out the banana crate covered in the old-fashioned, dark red prayer cloth, placed it against the wall of the mosque, and then sped off down the empty predawn main roads.

Turad did not read these details in the green file he found in the bus station. He was reading official documents, but then he got lost for a while in the realm of his imagination before ending with a long, deep sigh as he whispered to himself: You poor thing, dear foundling Nasir. Was your father, the taxi driver who owned the Cressida, called Abdulilah? Was your mother in the wide red blouse and the skirt with the black and honey-colored flowers called Salha? Did you have to spend the first night of your life in the street, and lose your eye when wild cats came out of the darkness to attack you, taking you for a piece of quivering red meat? Why weren't you inside a modern house with the fiery red flowers of the bougainvillea pouring over the wall? Why didn't you spend your first years driving around in a taxi, babbling to your mother and father? Damn the tribes and their evil customs. What good have the tribes done for me, Nasir my friend? Nothing. They said I was defective because I was without an ear, yet before that my reputation and courage had preceded me into the desert wilderness. This father of yours, my foundling, abandoned you, and ran out of your mother's life for the sake of the tribe. His lover's heart did not even flinch when your mother, who did not belong to a tribe, wept. He did not listen to her trembling young body when it taught him how to love and showed him new life, when he had been a boorish and uncouth brute who knew nothing of the world except Suad Hosni's smile, her half-closed eyes, and her hair pulled back like a horse's tail.

Stolen Manhood

"YOU'VE LOST YOUR EAR, MAN, BUT THE real problem is when someone loses his life and his future, his happiness and his stability." Amm Tawfiq fell silent as he sat on the high reed chair in the Café Emperor just outside of town. He took a long puff on his *sheesha*, and Turad listened to the bubbling of the water in the glass bowl at the bottom of the pipe. It was as if the *sheesha* were chuckling at them, mocking both of their fates.

"Do you know that the days on the ship were easier than these days now? After we pulled away from Sawaken, we spent days on the open sea. We put on the *ihram* pilgrim clothes before we reached the port. And I told you about that Eritrean man who pushed me on my face in the toilet and did it with me. I learned that everyone can do it with you dozens of times a day, in different ways, and with different meanings!"

79

Amm Tawfiq breathed a long sigh, but not a single tear dripped from his eye, lest it slide down the skin of his face, which hardly differed from the hide of an ancient and decrepit crocodile. It was as if there were no more tears in the lakes at the corners of his eyes, or if there were, then no longer enough time for him to weep. He was chatting late one summer evening, and since many of the café's patrons had already left, his swarming woes were uninterrupted except by the meanderings of the Indian waiter, whom they both called Yaqub because of the enormous resemblance they thought he bore to the goalkeeper for al-Tadamun and the national squad.

In his mind's eye Amm Tawfiq could still see, like some distant hazy dream, the bustle of an old port that ships could scarcely reach because the waters were so shallow. The boats would drop anchor more than two hundred yards from the jetty, and then the porters would jump into sailing skiffs and, with belts of leather or cloth tied around their waists, vigorously shove the animals down the smooth gangplank, which stretched down from the deck of the ship without steps. The sheep slid down, bleating loudly, accompanied by crates, sealed and stamped, carried by the porters, some filled with leather goods and folk remedies imported from Kurdufan, others full of spices and Indian sandalwood that was sold in the Shindi market. There were smaller boxes, too, but they were heavy and firmly locked, filled with Ethiopian gold from the Shindi market. And there were slaves: women, children, and men in their white *ihram*, driven into a line on the deck of the *African Moon* after she had been unloaded, who had been brought up from the hold to be transferred into the sailing skiffs. The little boats navigated their ways uneasily through the channels and coral reefs, until they reached more treacherous bits near the coast, where their cargoes were unloaded onto small dhows that slipped quietly and effortlessly up to the old customs dock. A group of men stood there. One of them held a ledger and had a black hat on his head. Other porters began to carry the merchandise from the small sailing boats onto the quay and, after the customs men had walked around and inspected them, from there to trucks with wooden sides. Slaves alighted from the last three vessels—men, women, and children wearing their *ihram*. They were ordered into a long line, which was soon broken up into small groups. At one end there were three children whose ages ranged between eight and eleven. One of them was called Hasan, but that would be changed to Tawfiq, which means "good fortune." His good fortune would head back out to sea, never to return; anguish and misfortune would follow him like his shadow for the rest of his life. When he walked it would move after him as if it were whipping him, and when he stopped to take his breath, misfortune would stop with him, clinging to him like preordained fate.

Voices and commotion mingled with the singing of the porters as they hurried down the gangplanks, their backs bent under the crates and sacks. From the edge of the port came men in short white *thobes* with belts around their waists and red turbans on their heads. They split up to look at the groups of slaves, and one of them headed toward the three black children. He looked at them through his small, sharp eyes. His beard was carefully trimmed. He told them he was the pilgrim guide. Then he hurried them along in front of him with a fat man who had enormous wobbling breasts, and who sputtered for breath as he tried to keep up with the three black children and the pilgrim guide. Outside, the sky was clear blue, and two huge trucks stood in the dusty street, one with brightly colored wooden sides. As they approached the vehicles the man with the sagging breasts yelled, "Yo, Rizg!" A huge man in his thirties peered out from the back of one of the trucks. He had a long drooping mustache. He extended his long arm to one of the children, and in one swift move heaved him up into the middle of the truck. In no time at all the three of them were inside.

Through the colored wooden slats on the side of the truck, Hasan—or Tawfiq—watched the fat man as he paid two pieces of silver to the pilgrim guide and climbed into the truck next to the driver. The pilgrim disappeared and the truck moved off, swaying heavily as it lumbered down the narrow alley between the decorated high walls and protruding wooden balconies of the houses. Some had *roashans*, ornately carved and covered in fine latticework, jutting out a little into the street, behind which women sang as they hung out their laundry. From one of the casements, wisps of smoke spiraled into the sky where a man and woman shared a *sheesha* and spied on the street below through the gaps in the woodwork.

At last the truck reached the end of an alley in the quarter of al-Mazlum, an old name that means "he who has been severely wronged." A minaret stood on the corner, and, after a number of desperate attempts from the driver, the truck turned right into a small square and came to a standstill. Through the slats in the side of the truck, Hasan (or Tawfiq) could make out some children skipping after the truck and singing a song he could hardly understand. The fat man stepped into the square and shooed the children away. A woman's voice, drawing out the words like music, came from one of the *roashans*: "Mohamaaaaad, Hasaaaaan, up here now!" The kids scattered in all directions. The huge man with the mustache opened the back door of the truck and pushed the black children out into the street, where they bounced around like rubber balls. Little

Hasan, who was to become Tawfiq, ended up flat on his face, and he sniffed the strange smell of the dust. He pulled himself to his feet in terror and ran after the other two youngsters across a narrow alleyway and into the doorway of one of the tall buildings, with the fat man and his pendulous breasts and the huge man with his flowing mustache and his sleeves rolled up over his burly arms in close pursuit.

The house with its five floors was amazing; the three youngsters were forever stopping, dazzled by the building and its passageways and stairs, its sofas and carpets, and its spacious lobby, which led into the main sitting room decorated with carved panels and expensive furniture. At the far end of the sitting room, two parallel stone stairways led to the upper floors, and to the left of the stairways was the door leading to the servants' bedroom and a bathroom and a storeroom. And in the far corner was the servants' staircase, narrow and dark.

"The huge man with the mustache"—and now Tawfiq takes up the story—"pushed us along with his bare arms until he shoved us into the storeroom, which was full of sacks and crates and tins of zinc. It resembled a narrow corridor and was crammed with spare things. I don't know why they put us there the first night and bolted the door behind us. Maybe it was because the storeroom was the only room without any windows, so we couldn't escape.

"The fat man gave us new names, after he had asked us our real names and said, 'No. Those names are no good.' He pointed at me: 'Your name's Tawfiq'; pointing at the others he said, 'and you are Anbar, and you are Jawhar.' We nodded in agreement. He looked into Anbar's eyes for a while and lifted his face with the tips of his fingers as he pondered a scar over his left eyebrow, the trace of a deep wound that had not completely healed. He drew closer, and with his finger pushed up Anbar's left eyelid and stared into his yellow eye. He grabbed Anbar's lower lip, pulling it down and looking at his teeth. Then he patted him twice on the back, and after he had gone off he sent us each a quarter loaf of bread, which we gobbled up with trembling hands we were so hungry. That night I didn't fall asleep until it was nearly dawn. I slept standing up because the room was so narrow, and in the morning I woke up to the smell of Anbar's excrement. He couldn't hold it in and had to do it squatting there like a stray dog in a space he'd made between two sacks.

"The next day I was on my own. The fat man and the man with the mustache came in with a black woman who looked to be middle-aged. She was saying, '*Ma sha'allah*, what lovely young men they are!' She rubbed our bare heads and inspected our backs and shoulders. She had a red scarf wrapped around her head and a gold ornament piercing her nose. From her wide mouth, which was full of gold teeth, came a strange odor that I later learned was the smell of *dayrman* tooth sticks. 'By God, they're excellent, Abu Yahya,' she said to the fat man, and from that moment I knew his name. They took Jawhar and Anbar to the bathroom. The woman went in with them, carrying two clean *thobes*, two white *ghutras*, and some towels. They locked me in the storeroom. I thought that Jawhar and Anbar would stay in one of the many rooms in the house, but I never saw them again.

"Her name was Umm al-Khayr, Mother of Goodness, and she was the housekeeper. I don't know where she stayed, but when I woke up from the stupor she looked after me like my mother. Ah, what a time it was! We don't know what ruler controls this world or what ruler makes a mess of it. I remember that day as if it were yesterday. I remember the face of the man who came into my room with a pair of glasses perched on his thick nose and secured by a black cord behind his ears. He had a metal case with him. It was small and weird looking, red, like he had brought it from Hell. It had pictures of minarets and domes and trees engraved on it. As the man opened the small black lock, Umm al-Khayr stood behind him next to the door. Her two eyes looked sad as she said, 'Don't be afraid, Tawfiq my boy. The barber's going to shave your head.' There were all kinds of tools in the bag: razor blades, cotton, white gauze, a bottle of cologne, a piece of Abu Anz soap, some matches and metal cones, and lots of other things I can't remember. What I can remember, though, are his hairy hands as he set out his tools with well-practiced precision. He slipped the razor blade into the lip of the shaver and quickly started to cut off my hair. Umm al-Khayr had disappeared off into the house. When my hair had fallen for the first time in this strange town, the man with the glasses tore off a small piece of cotton, rolled it into a ball between his fingers without looking at me, soaked it in a yellow liquid, and stuck it up my nostrils. A strong pungent smell sneaked directly up into my head, and I saw the walls begin to move. The man's face went all misty and seemed to hover around the room as if he were a genie. After that I couldn't see anything in front of me. I was so drugged I couldn't feel a thing, even though I could sense there was something going on lower down, between my thighs. All I could see was the Nile and the forests and the huts and Umm Kidada and Shindi and Umm Durman and Port Sudan and Sawaken, and my mother and my uncle, Fadlallah Adam, and his wife, Bakhita Osman, and Idris al-Sayyid the cripple and his wife, al-Sabr Zayn. I saw the faces of the slave traders, one after the other, in al-Bitana and

Kurdufan and Bahr al-Ghazal and Bantio and al-Fasher. I saw my mother washing me on the banks of the Nile one spring day with other women around her washing their few clothes. I saw my mother moving away and me tying two planks of wood together and pushing them out into the water and leaping on top of them like the mischievous child I was. I saw myself floating north up the river, and then I saw myself on the same two wooden planks bouncing over the waves out into the Red Sea heading east. After two or three days, maybe more, I awoke from the coma. I was laid out on a sponge mattress covered in a striped blue sheet. Next to me was a jug of water, cotton, and some Mercurochrome. I tried to get up, but I immediately felt incredibly dizzy, and my head fell back onto the crushed feather pillow. The point of one of the feathers pricked my neck like a needle. I lifted my hand and felt the pillow as I dreamed about all those feathers. I wanted to plant them in my arms and fly away, far away, into the west, until I was over the Nile. I tried to move but I felt a terrible pain in my bladder. Umm al-Khayr came in. She had the gold ornament in her nose and one of her rare smiles. I didn't know if she was Mother of Goodness or Mother of Evil. 'Welcome back, Tawfiq, my boy,' and she took a bottle from between my thighs where yellow urine had collected.

"'You'll find excellent work,' Umm al-Khayr told me. You'll be able to work in the palaces. You will know greatness and prosperity, and you'll be a rich man.' But I never became rich, and I wasn't a man anymore.

"I learned a few days later that I had been castrated, and that all I would use my penis for was to urinate. Imagine that, Turad: they tricked me over there with a piece of grilled fat, and I fell into the slave traders' trap, and here they tricked me with a small ball of cotton, which they shoved up my nose, and I fell unconscious. The first time I sold my humanity for the smell of gristle and became a slave, and the second I sold my manhood for the smell of cotton and became a eunuch. May God destroy all smells. If I didn't have a nose, Turad, if I'd lost my nose like you lost your left ear . . . Your left ear, by the way, you never did tell me how you lost it. Did somebody cut it off with a knife, or a razor?"

A Fight with
the Guards

NAHAR AND I WERE LIKE THE WILD ANIMALS of the desert. We could sniff our prey from far away, and would pounce on it brilliantly. We knew the desert—its dunes, hills, and sandy plains—like a man knows the lines of his own palms. We knew the places of pasture and abundance, the dry riverbeds, and the water holes. We made our way guided by cairns and stars, and we raced with the wolves and sought shelter with hyenas in their lairs. Many a time we'd choose a cave where we could rest and spend a night or more. True, we used to rob innocent people, true, we were thieves, but believe me, my brother Tawfiq, we never killed anyone unless our lives were in danger and we had to defend ourselves.

Turad and Nahar knew not only the roads they used to take and the places where the caravans stopped for the night, but also the times of their coming and going that greatly increased with the *hajj* season, when their booty and earnings were more abundant. They would wait in the darkness behind a hill or a rock, or beneath a huge acacia or *awshaz*, overlooking the spot where the line of camels would pass, whiling away the black night with tales of the desert, battles, and women. When Turad sniffed the caravan slowly approaching from many miles away, he'd tell his companion he could smell the men and the camels, and they would keep still, concealed behind a rock and holding each other's hand, for they could communicate by prodding and pinching their hands. As soon as Turad realized that the caravan was long and loaded with goods, and that there were few men and no weapons, he would tap Nahar's hand two times in quick succession as a signal to attack, but if he saw that the caravan guards were bristling with arms, he would prod the center of Nahar's palm with his middle finger as a sign of death, and they would crouch in their hiding place until the caravan passed.

On one occasion, at the beginning of the night with the crescent moon just over the horizon like the slender sculpted eyebrow of a sleeping woman, the scent of camels came upon them, like a herd in the desert. It invaded Turad's nose, and he motioned to his companion to be silent. They lay motionless in the sand like two rocks. They had tied bands of cloth around their waists to keep up their tattered *thobe*s for ease of movement. They had their sharp knives ready, for it was their intention to sneak up past the guards and slip into the middle of the caravan. Turad would cut the rope linking two of the camels in the train, while Nahar would slice through the rope two camels behind. Turad would then lead the two animals away from the caravan, and Nahar would tie the two ends of the rope back together. None of the guards would be any the wiser. No one would be killed nor any blood shed.

As the caravan drew near, their ears discerned no singing from the guards, indicating that they had indeed approached at a time when the men were taking a short nap, which guaranteed a greater chance of ease and success in their mission. Turad's eyes fell upon a red she-camel followed by a white, and he tapped his colleague's palm. The two of them rushed forward in the desert darkness like cunning wolves. They separated. Turad moved in ahead of the red she-camel, and Nahar walked next to the white one, awaiting a sign from his companion. As soon as Turad had cut the rope, he gave the signal and held the two ends of the rope in his hands so that Nahar might finish his task. At that moment Turad would lead the two she-camels quickly away and disappear behind a hill, followed by his friend.

For the first time in his life, Nahar made a mistake, as a result of which his day was to turn into a heavy

night devoid of stars. After Turad managed successfully
to cut the rope halfway between the two animals, he
kept hold of the two ends so the caravan wouldn't become separated and the guards realize that something
was amiss. Meanwhile, Nahar was busy with the rope
to the rear of the two she-camels. He was walking
with the caravan, sweat pouring from his brow and
the rope pulled taut between his teeth and his right
hand, while his left gripped the knife and sawed away
at the rope. But perhaps because he had taken just a
fraction too long, as soon as the rope came loose, he
tugged urgently at the camel behind so that he could
fasten its rope to the one in front, Turad having led away
the two stolen camels. Nahar had pulled the camel too
forcefully, and all the animals in the caravan lurched
forward to keep up, which drew the attention of one of
the guards at the rear. He galloped forward and yelled
at the top of his voice, "*Al-hanshal*, thieves!" The silence and tranquillity of the desert night was shattered,
and the caravan roused from its slumber. The men
leaped down from their mounts as Turad tried to get
away with the two she-camels. Then sensing the danger, he abandoned them and ran toward a ridge of sand
that lay parallel to the route of the caravan. Nahar fell
into the hands of the travelers, for they greatly out-
numbered him. One of them caught up with Turad,
leaped on his back, and brought him to the ground.

They began to fight. Turad was able to cut the man's arm with his knife, and warm blood gushed onto the dark desert sand. Then three men rushed Turad all at once. He tried to stab one of them in the stomach, but a huge club thudded into his back, and he fell to the ground. As he struggled to his feet, one of the guards, who was very heavy, knelt on top of him, grabbed his hands, and tied them fast behind his back.

Turad was led before the emir of the caravan, his hair disheveled, blood and sweat dripping from his mouth. The emir was a middle-aged man with a beard streaked with white, a long twisted mustache, and two sharp eyes like a hawk's framed by sharply arched eyebrows. He looked at Turad and Nahar from atop a light-colored camel as they cowered on their knees below him with their hands tied behind their backs. He knelt his camel, dismounted, and walked toward them. He peered into Turad's eyes, bending over slightly so that their faces were almost level. Then suddenly he spat forcefully in Turad's face, turned away, and walked back to his camel.

I had closed my eyes grudgingly, Turad remembered. I would have loved to spit in the face of their emir, so that he might know the taste of the bitterness of the men of the desert, but at that moment I was a coward. I was hoping he would pardon us, because he was an emir, well armed and surrounded by his men, and we unarmed and bound, and completely at his mercy.

Turad wiped his face, suddenly aware of the noise and bustle of the waiting room. A small crowd had gathered by the counter for passengers on the waiting list, and the ticket clerk had climbed on a chair and was shouting, "Would everybody please calm down. You will all get a place. Now, would you mind getting into an orderly line?" As soon as they had lined up, others started to join the line in the middle, or hand money to those near the front, asking them to get them tickets, which caused the chaos and fuss to start all over again.

Turad let his mind wander once again to hear the voice of one of the cameleers in the desert, on that route they called the Shafallah Trail, for along its edges there were lots of *shafallah* bushes, with their abundant branches spread out over the ground. The man stood behind them, and his dagger flashed in the darkness: "Shall we cut their throats, sir?" As the light-colored camel raised itself off the ground, the caravan's emir looked into their pleading eyes. "No," he said. "They do not deserve that we pollute our hands with their blood, as we are intending to do the *hajj.*" Turad's heart no sooner danced than the man continued: "Dig two holes for them in the sand and throw them in. Bury them up to their necks. Just leave their heads so they can breathe.

That way they will not harm passersby." With that his huge camel set off in the direction of the Kaaba, while his men began to dig by the side of the trail. After they had made two deep holes on either side of the track, they stood Turad in one and Nahar in the other, then poured the heavy sand over them until they were completely covered up to their necks. Then they departed. One of them turned back, and walking toward them he lifted up his *thobe* and doused Nahar's face with his urine, which he then turned on Turad just as the stream came to an end. And with a laugh he ran to catch up with the caravan.

Abused
as a Child

HE STARTED LIKE A BIRD AFTER HIS short nap in the waiting room. The voices of the travelers resembled the buzz of flies in the scorching midday sun. Turad looked at his hands and found that they still gripped the green file, like the fingers of a little boy would clutch the thumb of his father in a busy crowd. He tried to get up out of his seat, but he had pins and needles in his legs, and all of a sudden he slumped down on his backside. A small plastic bag fell out of the green file. He bent over to pick it up off the hard cold floor of the waiting room. He inspected it closely and felt with his fingers something firm, the size of a pomegranate seed, and something else soft and limp. At that point he decided to open the little bag, and he glanced around furtively more than once: No one was watching him.

A child, five years old, an English word on the front of his dark green T-shirt, is laughing merrily, holding a knife in his hand. On the table in front of him stands a cake covered in white frosting, with some red flowers and thin candles around the edge. The candles have just been blown out, and wisps of white smoke rise into the air. Behind the child are other children crowding around, clapping, and more happy smiling faces.

As Turad looked thoughtfully at the photograph of the little boy, he noticed the missing left eye, and while the boy raised the knife and shouted, the other eye glowed, reflecting the flash of the camera. Turad turned the photograph over and read, "Nasir Abdulilah's birthday, five years old, the Home."

What kind of birthday is that, my young gentleman? Is there an anniversary to commemorate the day you were thrown away and lost? Do you celebrate the day you were born in a banana crate and left on the corner of the street, without a possession in the world save two little shining eyes looking toward the dark sky, imploring Heaven to protect you from the vermin and the creepy crawlies and the animals and the people? All you found was dejection and everlasting disappointment. What special day are you celebrating? The day vicious stray cats attacked you to dine on your plump shining eye, and you let out an immortal scream into Allah's Heaven? But it did not reach Heaven. Your mother in her red blouse did not hear it, nor did your father in his Toyota taxi. None of those lingering in their deep sleep heard your cry for help. The whole earth did not hear you. Nothing paid heed to your plight save a branch stirring on the huge cinchona tree that leans languidly against the mosque of Abdullah Ibn al-Zubair. Ah, you trees, cinchona and binsyan, acacia and lotus, wave your branches to the world so that it sees me!

The five-year-old child in the embrace of a Filipina woman gazes in astonishment at the camera. She has her arms around him like a fence, and her legs restrain his movement. She is laughing saucily at the camera. On the back of the photo, Turad read, "Nasir Abdulilah and Filipina maid, Lumbai, at the Home."

The six-year-old child is wearing blue overalls with a white shirt and a yellow hat. His mischievous right hand is thrown around the neck of a fat woman who is laughing uncontrollably as she tries to fend him off. Turad turned the picture over: "Nasir Abdulilah with nanny, Gamalat. First day of school."

A young man, his mustache just sprouting, has his arms stretched out across the shoulders of two other young men. All three of them have around their necks a green spotted snake made of wool and stuffed with cotton. The young man to the left in the picture is holding up two fingers behind the head of the young man in the middle. The wan smile on his face is more akin to a sneer at his friend, whom he has made with his fingers into a donkey or a rabbit or some other stupid animal.

On the back of that photograph, Turad read, "Memories. Muhammad Abdullah, Nasir Abdulilah, and Khaled Abdulsalam." After he had had a good look at them all, Turad stuffed the photos back into the small plastic bag. As he did so, his hand came upon another very small bag. He removed it slowly and found inside a lock of soft black hair. On the piece of paper stuck to the bag was written, "A lock of Nasir Abdulilah's hair the day he started school." Another small bag fell to the floor, and when he picked it up he read, "Nasir's first tooth. Six years old." An ambivalent smile flitted across Turad's lips as he looked at the tiny tooth, which was a yellowish color with some brown decay at the root.

My friend, Turad thought, all the mementos you have are bits of your body. You don't carry a family tree with you. You don't have a lovely house with a *majlis* for the men at the front, with low couches and cushions lined up against the walls, where you could proudly hang your family tree in a gold frame, like people do in this country, for they are very proud of their ancestry. You have no father, only a tooth that fell out, and no mother, only a lock of soft hair. You have no brothers or sisters, only people like yourself, abandoned and deprived, who are captured for you in photographs taken

by a transient Egyptian nanny who hides your fish din-
ner in the evenings because she fancies it herself, and
gives you a cheese sandwich instead, and then tells the
social worker that none of you likes the smell of fish.

It wasn't only the animals roaming through damp
warm alleyways that abused your body. The nannies
and the maids didn't spare you their mischief or lech-
ery, either; your body wasn't safe in their charge, even
as a tender child. Bath times filled you with dread.
Lumbai, the Filipina maid, would scrub your body in
the bathtub, and her hands would work their way un-
noticed between your thighs, then her face and her
mouth, until your skin was raw and turned bright red.
In the end the doctor had to come and have a look at
it after you complained about the pain. A decision was
made to terminate Lumbai's contract after an investiga-
tion, during which she admitted her habit, with the
excuse that you had something rather large, different
from the other boys and Filipino men.

You have a big organ, and the Filipina ladies working at the home couldn't ignore it. It helped them while
away their loneliness and isolation. And Amm Tawfiq—
they chopped off his world between his thighs and left
him with a urinator, nothing more. You came into this
brutal world thanks to the chaos of nature and the lust
of your arbitrary father, Mr. Abdulilah, servant of God;
it might as well be said servant of Satan—there's no

difference. The women around you have been trying to repeat the tragedy. You could find yourself with a little creature of your own, mewing like a cat. Would his mother run away from the hospital and leave him to the nurses and midwives, or would she place him by the door of the mosque in a crate for bananas or oil or sanitary towels? Damn, Nasir ibn Abdulilah. Is there no one who will save you, pluck the fruit between your thighs and toss it into the rubbish bin in the quarter of al-Mazlum, or in al-Sadd al-Gharbi district, so that finally you will be free of those who interfere with you and have so wantonly abused you?

Moon Passion

"AFTER SOME MONTHS MY DEEP SCAR began to heal, and the devastating terror that had swept over me at that time receded. I forgot the incident as I forgot my own name. Now I am Tawfiq, in a strange and distant land, separated from my own country and name by a sea and jungles and wild animals and merchants and raiders and middlemen and ships and houses and trails and tracks and innumerable sorrows.

"This alien country was to be my country, her people my people. I would wear their clothes and eat their food, and I was to be at their service until the day I died, or so I understood. Abu Yahya, the fat man, had decided to lend me out to his neighbor the perfume-seller, who had a shop in the *souk* in the center of town. He had taken me to him twice to fetch some herbs and potions for his daughter, Khairiya. She had been laid up in bed for forty days after giving birth to a very beautiful little girl.

"Khairiya was a pale adolescent girl. Her breasts were two ripe fruits, and her soft, intelligent eyes flashed brightly between her dark lashes. Her fingers were long and slender and ended in red-painted nails. When she moved them in her dark room it was as if red moons were appearing unexpectedly from behind the clouds. She loved her mother a great deal, and saw her father only on Friday evenings, for he spent all day in his perfume shop, and when he returned at night she would have nodded off already like a child. He would kiss her forehead and cover her face with a white branch-patterned bedsheet.

"The perfume-seller's daughter was neither bold nor flirtatious, but she had not listened to the tales and warnings of the older folk. She had not realized the madness that she could bring upon her family and house if she took a chance on the night of the full moon and hung out her underwear on the clothesline. She thought that they were just stories the adults told to amuse themselves on moonlit summer nights, but in fact she really did get into trouble. She had given her underwear a good scrub in a tub full of soap suds, wrung it out with her own soft hands, and hung it on the clothesline on a night when the moon was completely full. Before going inside she stood for a moment to contemplate the roundness of the awesome silver moon. He was looking down at her madly, contemplating her charms, the roundness of her bulging thighs, her breasts surging inside her cotton nightgown. She looked at him without paying too much attention, but then suddenly she started, as she noticed him shamelessly exploring the details of her body, and she shuddered with fear as she felt him descend toward her underwear and sniff it with his silvery light. She ran back inside the house, unaware of what the full moon might do to her panties with the little red flowers on them, or her white bras.

"After two months Khairiya began to get dizzy spells, and she suffered nausea and constant vomiting. Then her mother noticed how quickly her belly had swollen. At that point the story of Khairiya, the moon, and the underwear spread through the alley. The young girls started to hide their underwear, not just from the moon but from the light as well, and from all eyes, the moon's, and the people's, even those of their own families.

"In a matter of months the story of the quarter of al-Mazlum was on everyone's lips. Even the old port was awash in it. All the locals and the foreigners had heard the story of Khairiya the perfume-seller's daughter, and the moon daughter, so named by the people after the child's father, the moon. Indeed, little Khadija was pale and plump, with a round face just like the moon.

"Khairiya needed a servant to see to her needs after her mother fell ill with her heart. Her heart had been fragile and trembling, and no sooner did she learn the truth about Khairiya than it weakened and gave out. As for the father, he no longer went out to spend long days in his perfume shop in the center of town.

"That's when Amm Abu Yahya spoke to me: 'Tawfiq, my boy, people are for people and neighbors for one another. Your uncle the perfume-seller is in need. Go and see what he requires.' So I went to live in the perfume-seller's house. I used to help Amma Khairiya with everything; she would hold my hand when she got up to go to the bathroom, and I would stay with her for ages in her room on the second floor. The room contained a carved wooden bed with a striped counterpane, and the walls were freshly painted. On the wall opposite the bed there was a picture in a gold frame of my uncle the perfume-seller when he was a young man, and on the wall opposite the door hung the Koranic verse al-Falaq, embroidered in shiny gold letters on black velvet.

"She did not seem at all bothered by my presence. She would even undo the buttons of her cotton nightgown in front of me, take out her firm white breast, and place her brown nipple in the little one's mouth. The baby would clutch it tightly while Khairiya looked wistfully through the carved wooden *roashan* at the light outside.

"After two full months of service, she hardly even noticed if I entered the room. Then one night I went and stood by her head. She was lost in thought, looking at a black-and-white photograph of a young man with a *ghutra* neatly arranged on top of his head, sitting with legs crossed on a high reed chair in a local coffee shop. When she saw me she flew into a rage, screaming at me not to creep up on her again or look secretly at her things. I was disturbed and went out of the room; I spent the whole day in the corridor. The next morning she called to me, 'Tawfiq, come here.' I went in. Her eyes were swollen and red. She pushed a ten-riyal note into my hand and whispered, 'Ya Tawfiq, don't tell any-one about that photo!' motioning toward the drawer of the bedside cabinet. I nodded my head. It did not occur to me at that point that there might be a link between the photograph and the moon that had smelled her pan-ties with the little red flowers on them. Instead, I shot off to the nearest street market, after I had found out where it was, and, passing the perfume and gold shops, I bought a white *ghutra*, which I arranged on top of my head like the locals do.

"After several months Amma Khairiya began to open up to me. She would ask me to keep her com-pany, and to make her green tea or tea with mint from al-Madina. She talked to me at length about her life and her boredom with the house and its four floors, which to her was more like a prison. She also talked about the treasure Abu Yahya al-Halawani had found. She said he used to sell pastries on the sidewalk. 'Imagine, Ya Tawfiq, this man who owns land and property and buildings used to be a humble pastry-seller; he didn't even have a shop. When he started off he used to lay out his wares on the sidewalk. Then he bought a wooden cart with wheels, and he put trays on it with glass covers, full of pastries. And now, Ya Tawfiq, after he used to shoo the flies from his pastries, he needs servants to shoo the millions from his face. And you know what? He told everyone it was the treasure he found.'

"I asked Amma Khairiya about the secret of the treasure. 'You know how there were people before us,' she said. 'I mean, centuries ago, really rich people who had gold and lots of jewels. Whenever they feared that raiders and thieves who used to threaten the country would come and steal their treasure, they went and buried it underground. And when the enemies attacked the country and killed the people, they found nothing worth mentioning, and they did not know that the gold and the treasure were underground. That treasure stayed underground for years, and no one knew where it was. Some local people, when they dug into the ground to build their houses, found the treasure, like Abu Yahya al-Halawani.'

"He owned one of the new quarters, which he had decided to call Al Halawani Development. That's all thanks to the treasure he found in bags stamped with the seals of tribes and peoples from long ago. They say that he gathered all the people of the quarter of al-Mazlum and threw three bags and a rusty casket among them, and said that he wanted to prove to them that he had discovered a part of the treasure of Solomon, or Goliath, or the treasure of Bani Hilal. When I was little I thought of running away from the perfume-seller and Abu Yahya and escaping into the desert to look for treasure buried in the sand. I believed the whole story, just like I believed at first that the moon had bedded Khairiya and sowed his seed inside her womb, and it had taken the form of a little girl of over-powering beauty who looked like the moon. Isn't it natural that she would look like the moon if he were her father? And like the other inhabitants of the quarter of al-Mazlum, I believed that the damn moon had done it after her panties hanging on the clothesline had led him astray. But I discovered the whole game when I found Khairiya hiding the black-and-white photograph of him wearing his carefully arranged *ghutra*. Sometimes she'd put it under her pillow, sometimes in the drawer of her bedside cabinet. Was that young man the moon? And were we—Jawhar and Anbar and I, and all those who had been snatched before us, and those who would be stolen after us—were we the treasure? The treasure that Abu Yahya had discovered, that made him burn his pastry cart, and his shop in the town center, to buy land and property with the price of us, and undertake new development projects in the country?"

Prisoners
of the Sand

OUR HEADS, NAHAR'S AND MINE, STUCK out above the sand like two stones in the desert night, like two black stones reflecting the moonlight. Damn moon, who slept with Khairiya, the perfume-seller's daughter, and who trod on our heads with his light, exposing us to all the wild beasts in the wilderness. Is it your light, Moon, that reveals our predicament in the sand, or is it the smell? That smell, the smell of roasting that led you, Amm Tawfiq, into the trap of the slave traders, the smell of the narcotic that sent your childhood into a haze so they could cut off your organ and the manhood that awaited you. That delicious smell, the scent of a woman's perfume that blew your father's mind, Nasir who was found in the street, and deluded your mother, Salha, so she gave him warmth and crazy convulsions in a dark back alley? Is it smell that cost Khairiya, the perfume-seller's daughter, so dearly, sleeping with the moon after she'd shown him her panties with the little flowers?

Is it smell—gorgeous, noble, and alluring, with its long intertwining strands like a spider's web—that trapped them all like flies? Is it smell, too, like a child leading a blind man down a dark road, that led the sightless wolves in the desert silence as they trotted along the Shafallah Trail, hurrying toward the stench of perspiration and fear? Sweat pouring copiously from the scalps of Turad and Nahar, revealing human scent and exposing the hapless prey to starving animals on the prowl?

What can we do? How do we get out of this one, brother? These were the questions they began to ask after the palpitations of the heart slowed down and their spirits stilled, while the smoldering brand of intellect burst into flames. Is there a solution or a way out? Nothing shone out in their minds, their hands tied fast, buried up to their necks in the heavy red sand. The same sand that they had embraced for so long became, that distant evening, their jailer, paralyzing their movement, holding them from roaming freely through the wilderness.

When Turad was alone in the desert, all the creatures were his friends. The sand served as his bed; the dune, the hill, and the plateau knew him well. The caves opened their hearts to him and offered him shelter.

The riverbeds and springs watered him and washed his body, the pasture lands and the fresh desert shoots recognized him when he passed. The acacia and the *awshaz* and the *sidr* offered him shade. The burning embers of *ghada* logs and *samr* roots kept him warm on cold desert nights. Not even the wolves thought to attack him, for they shared his food. Edging up to where he sat, he would throw them pieces of the game he had just hunted, and they would withdraw a little and stand on top of the hill, watching the moon without howling, which was not their habit. It was as if they were standing guard over him against misfortune or wild beasts and desert snakes. They even kept a watchful eye over him when other humans were about.

After he had battled with Nahar for hours and they were both exhausted, each of them discovered that he was merely engaged in combat with a hardened warrior and courageous fighter, and they decided to become friends, each protecting the other and defending him. From that time forth, Turad changed his relationship with the noble creatures around him. He mocked the sand and insulted the wadis and chopped the *awshaz* and acacias; he killed the hungry, panting wolves.

Turad remembered all of this, and the thoughts were like a wild wind raging violently inside his head that sprouted through the sand, the sand that was avenging its dignity, pressing down with all its weight on his body, surrounding him on all sides so that he could not move. Even the *shafallah* bushes stretched their branches arrogantly and yawned in disdain at Turad, betrayer of the trees, the desert shrubs, and the pasture and the wolves.

The *shafallah* bushes could have crawled on their bellies toward him and his friend, stretching out their foliage to conceal their heads from the hyenas, wolves, and snakes. The winds could have stopped driving their scent through the lowlands and over the mountains and hilltops. The sand could have alleviated their plight, shifting its weight from their buried bodies so that they might extricate themselves from its heavy embrace. The wolves, too, could have protected and guarded them as they had done in the past. But none of this happened. All creatures abandoned them, all conspired against them, and against their survival.

If some caravan or other were to happen along the Shafallah Trail, they thought, would it rescue them or turn away in fear and horror, seeing two heads sticking out of the sand like stones? If they asked the travelers for help, would they turn their backs, having made up their minds that these were two dwellers of the underworld. "Yo, fellow travelers, we are not genies. Come! Pull us out of this sandy grave; free us from its creeping onslaught, which is like the aggression of vipers. Rescue us, or we shall die of starvation, or fright, or fall prey to the animals."

As they whispered together, and the sweat dripped over their faces and down their necks in the desert stillness, they heard a long howl in the distance. It was an autumn night, and the winds were blowing, diffusing the smell of human in all four directions—five, in fact, if you included the sky, which during the day would be teeming with hawks and vultures.

The scent streaked like a snake across the sand, while the howl trembled on the breeze, and gradually drew nearer. As their horror increased, their sweat poured more profusely, and the eager winds transported the mannish smell to the muzzles of the wolves prowling in every corner of the land.

Then in the distance they spotted a wolf, hurrying through the darkness. He stopped, sniffed the ground with his snout, and stood for a moment before stretching his head into the air. He let out a piercing howl, then hurried toward them. Where are you going, wolf? What battle will you engage in with them? What kind of battle will it be if it isn't even? Between one free and unconfined, all his weapons at the ready, razor-sharp daggers in his mouth, pointed arrows at his feet, and those imprisoned in the sand, who possess neither their hands nor legs, neither strength nor a stick or club to ward off harm and wolves. Damn you, wolf! What malice do you hide behind your shining eyes? What depravity would make you take on two men stripped of all defense save their screams?

I remember one time the heavens opened, and Nahar and I took refuge in a cave. We smelled a scent we could not mistake; a wild animal had used the cave. We decided not to run away, but rather to settle the matter in its dwelling, and to stand and fight like men. I took a corner by the entrance, and Nahar took the corner opposite, carrying a sharpened dagger with death glistening on its edges. The place where I was crouching meant that anyone entering would have to pass me first, so I resolved to attack the wolf with my bare hands, and then Nahar would rush in with a thrust from behind. Our fear was that there would be more than one, but the evidence we found indicated that the wolf was alone.

When the wolf entered, its smell and breath preceded it. It, too, was apprehensive, as if it had smelled human scent. Letting out a piercing scream that resounded around the cave, I leaped upon it and grabbed its snout. It tried to struggle free and flailed its left paw at my shoulder, tearing at my forearm with its claws and leaving lines of blood. Nahar attacked from behind with the speed of lightning and cut open the beast's belly with his knife. Its intestines poured out, and it fell to the ground, its legs in the air like a bloated corpse.

Now, Nahar, it's not the same story. The hands with which I grabbed his muzzle, the repository of his razor-edged daggers, are now tied behind my back deep inside the sand. And so your hand, that bravely brandished the dagger, is also bound with ropes and buried beneath the sand. Nahar, have you ever seen a more desperate and dreadful death than this? For your enemy will display such artistry as he kills you, putting you to death with great deliberation, savoring each mouthful as he devours your face organ by organ, and each time he lunges, you will scream with all the strength your tongue can muster, for its turn is yet to come.

The Journey of
Thorny Dreams

"I WAS SAD. THE SUN WAS DRAWING ITS golden mantle across the shoulders of the houses in the quarter of al-Mazlum. They had just pushed me into the back of a Ford truck with a pile of furniture and household items: rugs and blankets, and pillows with colorful linen covers. I took one and placed it under my head as we drove along through the darkness. It was stuffed with feathers, and the sharp quills scratched my face. Ah, if only I could put the feathers along my arms and fly. Slowly I would ascend, little by little, until I was a bird in the open sky. I would cross the Red Sea and circle over the Nile. I see it now—the women standing along its banks, washing their pots and pans, scrubbing clothes, and singing. I see the naked children in the river, splashing one another and swimming. Onward I fly and see the forests and jungles, I see the huts of small scattered settlements, and I see the slave drivers mounted on swift horses, some holding sharp spears, others aiming rifles and firing. I see the slave traders marching a herd of slaves to the Shindi market. I see my mother escaping through the bush and her master, Ahmad al-Haj Abu Bakr, as he rapes her again and again. I see the Eritrean man pushing me on my face and shoving his cock up my backside until I almost choke. I see Bakhit trying to escape from the slave traders and the bullet whizzing through the dry forest air and thudding into his back. I was a bird in the sky over Sudan until one of the slave traders pointed his rifle at me. A fearsome bullet came speeding toward me, and I couldn't avoid it. The white feathers scatter into the sky as they fall off my body, and I plunge to the ground, a lifeless corpse."

The Ford jolted along some rough dusty track, heading east. In the back Tawfiq slumbered indifferently, a child who does not know what fate has in store. Frightful dreams and nightmares accompanied him, and the smell of *sheesha* coming from the old coffee shops outside the town hovered around him. A few days later he found himself in a new and unfamiliar city. He ended up in a huge palace, which differed greatly from the houses with many floors and *roashans* he had known in the quarter of al-Mazlum. The green expanses and the luxuriant trees surrounding the palace were the first things that he noticed. It was these gardens that he was to work in later on as a gardener. But first, for the years of his childhood and adolescence, he worked in the palace as a servant, side by side with a number of slave girls who serviced the many wings. He was allocated to the wing of Amma Madawi, as an assistant to two slave girls, Zahra and Umm Kalthum. Zahra, or Zuhayra, as they always used to call her, was just a few years older than he was. She was black and smooth skinned with protruding breasts, like suppressed anger waiting to be released. Her lips were full and ripe, just ready to pop open like a freshly picked fig. In fact, they did pop open one afternoon in the pantry, after she had called young Tawfiq to help her move some sugar, tea, and coffee into the kitchen. In the commotion of the sacks and chests piled on top of one another, she fell upon his lips and urged him to pluck that ripe fig of hers.

He learned a lot at her hands, and he yearned for more before he tasted the ultimate disappointment. He was busier than he'd ever been. He'd walk past her while she was making the beds, or seeing to the curtains and the valuable paintings and marble statues with an ostrich feather duster, or wiping them with a cloth, and he'd leave one hand free to caress and explore her huge backside, but she wasn't interested anymore. She'd found out he was a eunuch one night when she got all hot and horny and was waiting for him to

shove it inside her. "You're only good for pissing!" she
yelled angrily.

He was thirteen, four years younger than she was,
when that happened. From then on Tawfiq withdrew
into himself, and maintained a stubborn silence through-
out the subsequent years. He was overjoyed when
Amma Madawi decided to take him on as her chauffeur. She had gotten married, and when she moved to
another private palace, Tawfiq went with her. It was
the first major chance he had had to put behind him
the tragic wound that raged whenever he made eye
contact with Zuhayra.

When Zuhayra divulged Tawfiq's secret to her companion Umm Kalthum, Umm Kalthum never left the two
of them alone. Perhaps Zuhayra had urged her friend
not to let Tawfiq be alone with her, so that she would
not waste her time with him. She wanted to be completely free to pursue her new dream, to fulfill her lofty
ambition of having her master's child in order to guar-
antee herself a stable life and a secure future. Tawfiq
also began to avoid meeting her in the rooms of the
palace, or even in the corridors for that matter, and he
looked away dejectedly whenever their eyes met.

He had never dreamt he would become a personal driver and enjoy some favor with his mistress,
but perhaps fate had had a role, too, playing the final
card in the life of her previous chauffeur, Anwar

Abdulnabi. They had changed his surname, Servant of the Prophet, to Anwar Abd Rabb al-Nabi, Servant of the Lord of the Prophet, for it is not common or indeed permissible to worship a prophet, for the only object of worship is Allah, may He be glorified. At least that's what they taught Anwar many years before they fired him.

Anwar was a young man in his thirties with a thick mustache. He was adept at arranging his astonishingly white al-Attar *ghutra* on his head, crowned with an extremely thick *igal*. He would start the engine of the Rolls-Royce, stand by the back door on the side opposite the driver's seat, and wait for several minutes, which sometimes could extend to a whole hour or even more. As soon as he smelled the seductive scent of a woman's perfume floating through the air, he would briskly open the back door without glancing in Amma Madawi's direction, then close the door behind her after she had sat down, taking care to gather up the edge of her black, embroidered *abbaya* so that it didn't hang over the beige leather seat.

How Anwar Abd Rabb al-Nabi rushed around with the mistress's two ladies-in-waiting, Buthayna and Safiya, when they were accompanying her to open and close doors for her, until in the end she decided that this would be Anwar's task alone. He boasted about the recognition all over the palace.

It would not be easy for Anwar to forget that ill-fated evening, which was to be the beginning of the end of his working life. He had prepared himself for an official function she was planning to attend, the opening of an exhibition of paintings by young women abstract painters. At seven o'clock, an hour before the appointment, he had parked the lime green Rolls by the main entrance. After a long wait, by which time it was almost nine o'clock, an hour past the starting time, he felt a sudden cramp in his stomach so severe that he could hardly stand up, and he made a run for the outside toilet. She came out of the palace at that exact moment and didn't find him there to open the door for her and her lady-in-waiting Buthayna. What made matters worse was that she remained inside the car for almost five minutes before he reappeared. He got in all flustered, thought to offer an apology or some excuse for his negligence, or to explain to her the overwhelming circumstance that had forced him to the toilet, but he didn't utter a word. It worried him that she didn't say anything, either, or curse him, or direct her usual instructions to Buthayna as to what her duties would be during the opening ceremony.

Two days after this incident, just a mere two days, he had taken the liberty, while waiting for her to emerge from a social function, to cross the street and buy a packet of Marlboro Lights. As he was waiting for the shop assistant to give him his six riyals change, he spotted her out of the corner of his eye getting into the car. He dove out of the shop, leaving his change with the assistant, ran across the busy road, almost getting himself run over by a speeding white Caprice Classic, got into the Rolls, and started the engine in a fearful muddle. Minutes after she'd entered the palace the order came to withdraw the keys from Mr. Anwar Abd Rabb al-Nabi and hand them over to Tawfiq, along with notice that the services of the former be terminated forthwith, and that he receive all monies owing to him.

True, Tawfiq did know something about driving cars, but this was very different. Driving a magnificent vehicle like a Rolls-Royce was not the same as driving a Toyota pickup, and carting about a few bits and pieces in the back was not the same as having the honor of conveying the mistress to her social functions.

Previously Tawfiq had stopped the pickup at the outside gate to ask Abu Loza, who was wearing his olive green cap with the two woolen earpieces on the side, "Do you need anything, Ya Badawi?" The Bedouin, Abu Loza, would slowly strut out of his guard box and lean against the half-open car window: "Where you going, man?" They'd have a little joke, exchange a curse and a sarcastic laugh, and then Abu Loza would ask him to fetch some sweet *tahina* and some white cheese, a half pound, and not to forget the Vicks eucalyptus, either.

After Tawfiq the chauffeur went out on his first official mission in the lime green Rolls, Abu Loza was unable to enjoy their sarcastic banter anymore. All he could do was stand to attention and salute at the darkened rear windows, not knowing if there was anyone sitting in the back, or if anyone could see him from behind the darkened glass. Even if the people inside had noticed his habitual military stance, it was unlikely they would have been able to distinguish between him and his wooden guard house, between the box and the wooden salute.

Sin and
Punishment

"I USED TO DREAM OF BEING A SOLDIER. Ever since I was a child in the orphanage, I've loved military uniforms. In the home they used to call me 'the soldier.' Gamalat, the Egyptian nanny, used to call me Colonel Nasser. She hated President Gamal Abd al-Nasser. She used to curse him with or without good reason. Salma, the social worker, and Jawahir, the psychologist, used to egg her on. Gamalat would pretend to know all about him and inform them that he had eaten the Egyptian people and destroyed the economy. Social worker Salma would say that he wasn't only an enemy of the people, but that he was an enemy of Allah and Islam as well. Psychology specialist Jawahir would add that he was mentally ill, a megalomaniac, and suffered from psychological complexes.

"By giving me the nickname Colonel Nasser, Gamalat was showing that she hated me. She was saying that President Abd al-Nasser was a foundling and aggressive like me, and that I was obsessed with military dress because I loved to boss people around and was a little tyrant, and that I hit the other kids in the home."

In the waiting room Turad's eyes followed the lines of bad handwriting in the exercise book inside the green file. It was Mr. Nasir Abdulilah's diary. He turned the page:

One day a huge Egyptian woman came along with nanny Gamalat. I heard Gamalat yelling, "Ya leader, Ya Abd al-Nasser. Where do you think you're going?" I was heading for the water cooler without asking her permission like the other kids did. They asked permission for everything, to have a drink of water, to throw some rubbish away, to go to sleep, to go to the toilet, and, and, and. Why don't we behave like everyone else? Why do we ask permission to do everything, big or small? Why don't we feel we're like everybody else, that we're at home, in our own homes, and behave spontaneously like they do? When I heard her screeching in the corridor, I turned around, and the huge woman who was with her saw me, and she laughed as she looked at my missing eye and said for everyone to hear, "That's not Abd al-Nasser. It's Moshe Dayan.

Why, just look at his eye!" They roared with
laughter until tears ran down their cheeks. I filled
the blue plastic cup with water and drank, and
then went back to my family's room, while they
carried on having a good laugh.

It's not enough that when I was born I was
thrown into a banana crate and left near the
Abdullah Ibn al-Zubair mosque. It's not enough that
stray cats in the street had assaulted me, and I
could only cry my heart out. It's not enough that I
don't know who my father is, or who my mother
is, or who my brothers and sisters are, or where
they are right now, and why they haven't come to
take me. It's not enough that I was insulted in
school, or that I don't have a surname with the
definite article, which only goes to prove that I'm
unacknowledged and indefinite. It's not enough that
I was deprived of my dream and ambition to become a soldier, for the system doesn't allow me to
do that. None of that is enough, ever! But then, to
be called a dictator and a tyrant by those two
thieves just because I wanted to be a soldier. They
weren't satisfied with that, though. They made me
an Israeli, a Zionist, and a murderer, because I had
no one to defend me or to protect my eye from
harm while I was in the cradle. Aaaaah! If only I'd
lost my eye in the war, I'd have destroyed you

both with a shell. I'd have blown your heads off, you two thieves, before I lost it.

Anyway, what can we do? Today I wanted to record the story of my leaving the home and my going back again. Some children, of course, leave the home after real families have adopted them. They call them foster families, and they live with them like their own children. Quite often they suffer from abuse, are forced to do hard work, and are exploited. We hear this from our brothers who return with their minds and their bodies scarred.

One day a wealthy lady came to the home. She was met by the people in the nursery: the director of children's homes, the general supervisor, the undersecretary, and many others. They said she was an extremely prominent person; she was accompanied by elegant attendants. She went on a tour of the family sections. She played with the children and hugged and kissed them. Photos were taken to commemorate the occasion. I was one of the little children she played with, and she asked me pleasant questions: "What's your name, sweetheart? How old are you? Have you been to school?" All the usual questions.

Two days later I was surprised to find them arranging my clothes and papers, and holding a simple farewell party for me with my brothers in the family. I left with a black driver in a strange and magnificent car. All through the journey I looked at the gold door handle. I put out my hand toward it, and a beautiful dark-skinned woman with a wonderful smell touched my arm. "Don't do that, dear!" she said. I looked at her, and then at the driver, and I didn't know if she was talking to me or the driver. Then she chatted to keep me occupied for the rest of the journey. "My name's Buthayna. What's your name?" And with great shame and embarrassment I said "Nasir," but because I don't pronounce the "s" very well, it comes out like a "th," making it sound like the word for spread. "Nathir," she mimicked back immediately. "Nathir what?" Then she laughed and hugged me to her breast, and it smelled like gardens and flowers in the morning.

She moved me away from her breast a little and addressed the driver: "Amm Tawfiq, don't forget to go by the supermarket. We need a few things urgently." She took a piece of paper out of her dress and handed it to the black driver, whose name I had just learned was Amm Tawfiq.

My room in the huge palace was the size of three family rooms in the nursery. Even the bathroom, my own private bathroom, was bigger than the family room that eight of us kids had lived in. Sometimes our mother was Gamalat the Egyptian and sometimes Lumbai the Filipina. As for our father, Baba Said, he would come and pick us up in his car or the ministry car and take us for a quick spin. On the way back we would always drop in at the Panda supermarket.

The first evening, Amma met me in one of the large reception rooms. She sat me down and stroked my head and caressed me as she said:

"Your name's Nasir, isn't it?" I nodded my head shyly.

"Do you know who your mother is?"

"Gamalat," I told her. She shook her head.

"Salma," I said, meaning the social worker. She shook her head again. "Jawahir," I suggested, who was the psychologist.

"No," she said. "I am your mother, my dear," and she pulled me close and gave me a big hug.

The first days in the palace were extremely difficult. How to sit at the table, how to put the napkin on my lap, how to hold the spoon and fork, how to eat. Where to start and where to finish, and how to stand up and leave the table. How to walk through the large rooms of the palace, how to speak to others, how to smile, and how to pronounce words in English—"Okay!" and "Good morning," and "Hi!"—with the vowel drawn out as long as possible. How to say "Thanks a lot" while allowing a smile of gratitude to form on my lips. How to say "Ma'am" and kiss her hand every morning.

I learned with great difficulty when and how to go to the toilet, and to stay there for ages. I learned to take my bath at a leisurely pace, with the assistance of Buthayna or Safiya. Even if I wanted to go out into the garden to play and have fun, I had to do it in an orderly fashion, not chaotically. Good Lord! How can I play without stirring up the dust, dirtying my clothes and shoes, or throwing my bicycle in any old corner of the palace? I longed for the old gardener not to keep such a close eye on me so I could break some shady branches off the trees, chase the squawking birds, and throw stones at the cats with the really soft fur.

What a sad and sorry ending I came to in that miserable palace. And whose fault was it? It was that old gardener's, carrying his shears and moving about among the lush gardens like a heavy nightmare. I was playing one Thursday morning, wearing a purple tracksuit with the Pink Panther's face on the front. I was holding the hem of my tracksuit top between my teeth to make it into something like a basket and was running beneath the trees, collecting fallen leaves and dry flowers and putting

them on the Pink Panther's face. Suddenly I felt my
bladder was going to burst. I looked left and right,
pulled down the elastic waistband of my tracksuit
bottoms, and relieved myself under the tree. I had
hardly begun to feel the relief when I heard the old
gardener yelling at me. He pounced on me, grabbed
me by the ear, and took me out of the garden.
Then, gripping me by the forearm, he led me inside
to where Ma'am was thumbing through the day's
papers. Proud and triumphant, he informed her of
my offense and awaited his reward. She motioned
to him with her eyes to leave, then asked me,
"Why? Don't you have your own private bathroom?" I wanted to tell her: "Indeed I do, I have
my own private, luxury bathroom, but I felt the
liquid building up in my bladder. What was I to
do?" But I didn't say a word. I just stood there,
hanging my head in shame, while she killed me
with her silent stare, which was tantamount to a
real flogging with a whip.

I had to leave the paradise of the huge palace
after that vile and disgraceful act, and come back
down to earth to my friends and brothers in the
orphanage. It was two or three days after the
garden incident, maybe more, I don't remember
exactly, when the Ethiopian driver took me to the
pickup truck. He'd piled all my stuff in the back

without me noticing. We drove along many streets until we reached Hayy al-Ghamita, where the home was. They opened the door, but I refused to get out of the car. They tried several times. I was crying my eyes out as I clung to the door handle of the pickup and screamed: "By Allah, I repent. I won't do it again. Take me baaaaaack!" I promised them I would never urinate in the palace garden again. But the caretaker, with the help of the black driver, was able to get me out of the car and drag me, thrashing, into the home.

The caretaker was extremely upset as he dragged me inside the orphanage, like you would a piece of dead game or a victim to the altar. The Ethiopian driver's face, on the other hand, was cruel and malicious as he peeled my hand off the door handle, as if he were getting rid of something evil and unclean, or a stubborn insect. He wasn't kind or sensitive like Amm Tawfiq. I wish it had been Amm Tawfiq who'd taken me back to the home. He would have reassured me, even if it wasn't true, that I'd just be visiting, and he'd come back in the evening, or the next day, to take me back to the palace.

Resignation
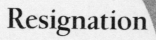

"AFTER I'D GOTTEN OVER THE TRAGEDY of those bitches, Zuhayra and Umm Kalthum, and their conniving and sarcasm, I moved to the new palace. Fortune had stood by me like a decent fellow, and I had become the personal chauffeur of the mistress. At last I began to experience some peace and security. Then, after the death of the old gardener, Marzuq, I lost my job as driver and took his place in the palace gardens.

"I was told, 'You're no longer any use as a driver. You're too old. The most suitable work for you is to be a gardener in the palace grounds.' And just as I had received the keys of the Rolls-Royce from Anwar Abd Rabb al-Nabi, I handed them over to the Ethiopian driver, Ahmad, and took up my last job before the grave, for hadn't old Marzuq pegged it. That's what life was like here. Inside the palaces, every creature has a defined role in life. Once that role is finished, his life there finishes. How miserable and depressing was my role, Anwar's, and Marzuq's? Ahmad's role, Abu Loza's, and others'? But the worst of all our roles was that of little Nasir. He was brought into the palace to be the adopted son. Mistress couldn't have children, and she had gone for many years without giving birth, but the maternal instinct was overwhelming, and she desperately wanted a child. She had to satisfy the desire in the quickest way possible, by driving the lime green Rolls to the orphanage. That's when some serious bad luck stepped into your life, little Nasir. You weren't lucky like some of the kids and the specialists thought you were. No way! You played a limited and temporary role. It ended as soon as Amma felt the first cravings of her pregnancy, and you, little Nasir, returned to your home, like I returned to the gardens, which looked just like the forests and jungles along the White Nile.

"You go back now, little Nasir. The real son's arrived. You can go, pseudoson, offspring of cats and stray dogs, you can go to Hell. It will be big enough for you, whether it has three doors, or seven, or twenty-one. Hell will contain your grief and your lost childhood.

"After years of pruning branches and cutting grass, of sadness and boredom, the royal decree proclaiming the emancipation of the slaves was issued. So I didn't die in the shade of a tree like the old gardener Marzuq.

I had to walk out of the palace gate carrying the deed of my freedom and wander about the streets and alleyways without owning my daily bread, or possessing any skill or trade from which to make my living. I was no good at anything, except that I could drive a car, but I was too old for that; or I could cut trees in Riyadh, and trim her long sadness.

"All I had preserved in my decrepit memory were the nights of a distant, half-forgotten childhood. I looked at the streets and saw only the banks of the Nile. The smells of the car exhaust were the smell of the river birds. I heard the hum of the engines and the beep of the horns as a distant song. I heard the voices of forgotten singers. I don't know why I suddenly remembered them so clearly. Khalil Farah was singing, and Surur and Kuruma and others. One of their voices rose above the rest in a wonderful sad solo:

> Darling, write to me
> And I'll write to you
> About my news and yours
> My news is longing and desire
> I spend the night with sighs and moans
> And remember our sitting on the hill
> Holding the cup of love to each other's lips
> I smile at you and you smile back

To the strains of the flute
And I my love
All my life I'll sing to you.

"The voice grew gradually louder, and the streets of the city seemed empty and unfamiliar. I could hear the voice, and see . . . see the women dancing, their succulent bodies swaying, see the men's faces glowing, dancing with them. Aaaah, Ya Tawfiq, what was it that brought you here?

"After staggering around the streets and shopping centers for two days, I went back to the palace and asked if I could stay temporarily while I sorted out a job that would keep me together in those dark oppressive days. That wasn't emancipation! What freedom could I enjoy after my whole life had gone by without a career, or a wife and children to keep me company in my loneliness and isolation? I was like a bird who doesn't fly away when the cage door is opened for him. It is not because he doesn't understand freedom, or that his wings are incapable of flight. No, that's not it at all. He is wiser and more intelligent than that. He has learned in the cage that seeds and water come to him. How can he provide for himself outside the cage if he has never learned how to before?

"One morning I decided to leave the palace for good. I went out through the gate that Abu Loza had spent more than two years guarding before he was also kicked out—sorry, I mean, before 'his services were no longer required.' I thought I'd get a job as a porter on the docks, but when I went there I found the place full of Asian workers. I left and told myself I'd get a job as a sales assistant, but I wasn't qualified: I didn't have a clean, fair, Lebanese face to entice female customers into the clothes shops or the perfume and cosmetics stalls. I thought about working as a laborer, a builder, or a tiler, but I wouldn't be able to compete with the Pakistanis, nor would I be accepted by them. I decided to look for a building and work as a doorman. That's what I decided, and I worked for a year and a half before the owner sold the building. The new owner got rid of me—sorry, my 'services were no longer required'—after he hired a cheap Bangladeshi worker to take my place.

"After that I got a job through a Sudanese friend who worked as an accountant in a ministry. I started off as a messenger, and then became the coffee boy. I spent years dragging my heavy body around the offices, bearing a silence and a deep secret inside me, which I never divulged to anyone.

"I wasn't like Turad the Bedouin fellow who got himself entangled in all kinds of buffoonery with some of the low-life staff. I always put up a barrier between myself and them, even though most of them did call me

Amm Tawfiq, perhaps out of consideration for my age, or my silence, which I think perplexed them a little.

"The first time he came into the room where I prepared the coffee, he shook my hand and said, 'I'm Turad, the new messenger in financial administration.' I welcomed him with an impassive face, but then after he visited me in my room in al-Murabba district, I began to feel that his features were not unfamiliar, as if we'd had a laugh together or shared a joke once a long time ago. After many questions about life and the jobs we'd done, I knew who he was the moment he said, 'I worked as a soldier, not a soldier exactly, but I was a guard at some big shot's palace gate.'

"I suddenly yelled, 'Abu Loza!' and embraced him heartily. Although he seemed unmoved, and didn't share my joy in finding a friend, he provided me with some company in my lonely, miserable life.

"Over many nights I told him my story from the time we had scattered and fled from the slave drivers, then fell into their hands again and moved around with them, passing through the Shindi market, Barbar, and the port of Sawaken on the Red Sea. I told him about my life in the quarter of al-Mazlum, being sold to Abu Yahya al-Halawani, and my castration. I recounted my working for the perfume-seller and his daughter, Khairiya, traveling here, and then working in the palaces as a servant, driver, and gardener. Turad, or Abu Loza, listened to me in amazement. Then he sadly told me the tale of his courageous exploits as a proud highwayman, how he fell in with his dear friend Nahar, and how the guards of a _hajj_ caravan caught them. I wondered how people undertaking the pilgrimage could commit such atrocities. What kind of _hajj_ were they hoping to make? They took me from my mother's arms, kidnapped me, and brought me to this country on the pretext of the _hajj_. You, Turad, lost your friend Nahar, and your ear, which caused you such pain and heartache, thanks to pilgrims going on the _hajj_. Would they perform a sincere _hajj_, free from obscenity and iniquity, to return to their homes as pure as the day their mothers bore them, with their sins forgiven and their efforts acknowledged? What effort would they be thanked for after they broke our spirits and stole our manhood? Tell me now, Ya Turad, finish off your story. Let's while away the Riyadh night with stories and sad memories, while the city sleeps like a fat old woman."

The Heroism
of the Wolf

TURAD LOOKED AROUND THE WAITING room for the owner of the green file. How did a file containing official papers find its way here? he asked himself. How did it leave the shelves and filing cabinets of the government department dealing with the case? Was this person, Nasir Abdulilah, the same Nasir that Amm Tawfiq talked about? It must be him. Didn't I just read in his diary that they took him from the orphanage to live inside a palace and to be their son? Didn't he talk about a black driver called Tawfiq who drove a lime green Rolls-Royce? Why don't I remember him from the time I worked as a guard at the palace gate? Could he have come after me or before me? I don't know. Anxious thoughts went around and around in the mind of this Bedouin fleeing from the violence of the city. In the desert you can see your enemy in front of you, he thought, and you can take him on in a fair contest. But the curse of the city, which is no different from Hell, is that you struggle against unknown enemies, enemies you can't see with your naked eye. Can we struggle against the firewood of Hell that devours us whether we are decent or wicked? I don't think so.

In that same waiting room Turad pursued his memories, like a puppy chasing its wagging tail. The scene of the two of them, him and Nahar, was still before his eyes, buried up to their necks in the gloomy Nafud desert. It occurred to him that the red swathes of sand, made even redder by the setting sun, were no different from the vermilion pits of Hell.

The drops of sweat trickling through their hair and down their necks were not for fear that they might die of thirst while they stood buried in the remorseless sand, but rather because they sensed that the moment of vengeance had arrived. Why not? For the signs were appearing gradually, from the *shafallah* bushes that crept around them but did not give a damn about their fate, to the wind, which did not keep their human scent to itself but intentionally cast it abroad to every wild beast in the wilderness. All that remained now was for the beasts to appear. They would not protect them from afar, nor contemplate the spectacle of their awesome strength and courage, but feast upon their warm and waiting flesh.

Here is the hoary wolf trotting down from the rocky outcrop overlooking the Shafallah Trail, sweeping the ground with his muzzle for the smell of man that drifts out tantalizingly over the sand. How many times had that wolf accompanied Turad on his forages and battles, and nights spent by the *ghada* fire, as he roasted the game he'd caught with his own hands? The wolf would spend the evening close by him, and then, when Nahar tossed him a piece of the prey, he'd pick it up in his teeth and hurry off into the night, only to reappear the next morning.

This time Turad's hands wouldn't be lighting the fire. They wouldn't be turning the meat as it cooked, or tossing the wolf his share. This time Turad was a prisoner with no right to defend himself, like one tied to the tent pole as words of rebuke rained down onto his face, his chest, and his stomach—onto every part of his body. All he could do was spit out blood, sadness, and bitter defeat.

The wolf came. Nahar whispered in undisguised terror and a broken voice. The wolf was a few steps away, walking like a blind man led by the sense of smell. When he saw their heads protruding above the cruel sand, he moved his body back a little and lowered his head toward the ground, as if he wished to conceal himself from his prey. He observed them for a moment before moving forward, his belly almost touching the sand. He froze awhile in front of Nahar, and looked into his eyes, a keen, cruel look; he did not avert his glare for a second. Suddenly he pounced and struck with his front leg. Nahar screamed as he pulled his face away. The wolf moved in with fangs unleashed like death and tore at him. Nahar howled as he struggled to move his face from the wolf's onslaught. He howled till the sand turned pale, and the acacia trees wept far away, and the *shafallah* bushes closed their eyes and shrunk back in shame, and the sand tried to release its grip on their bodies, but there was no time to free them from a starving desert wolf.

Portions of Nahar's plump face began to disappear. The wolf tore away his left cheek and then bit off his nose amid screams that uprooted the desert trees with grief. His shouting caused the pastures, the water holes and ravines, and the wadis to pray for him. The *awshaz* trees spread their branches toward the heavens in supplication. The lizards and scorpions, and the birds hovering in the sky and sleeping in their rocky nests, beseeched for intercession, but heaven did not stir, for it was immersed in a profound and overflowing slumber.

The moment the wolf devoured Nahar's mouth and lips, and snatched the tip of his tongue, the sacred screaming stopped. When the beast removed the windpipe with his incisors, Nahar's head slumped heavily to one side like a ripe fruit hanging ponderously from a branch, and then fell lifeless and discarded. But his spirit flew howling through the desert night, striking the trees, sand, and rocks, weeping, pursuing the caravans, travelers, and *hajjis*, questioning them, pulling the tails of the camels, surrounding the men, and weeping. Upward toward the distant heavens his soul soared, screaming at the smiling sleeping stars, extinguishing their glow with its hands. The stars were no longer lanterns adorning the night sky. Nahar's soul had put them out as it fled across the wilderness and through the heavens revealed in their nakedness.

With his oppressive hunger sated, the wolf circled the remains of Nahar while Turad, terrified, gushed sweat from his head. Turad had decided inside himself not to scream or howl or utter a single word. What would be the point? He closed his eyes and tried to sow composure in his heart. The wolf heaved his sluggish body around Turad while Turad waited, eyes shut tight, for a blow to take off his face, a swipe with a cruel razor-sharp claw, the bite of teeth with points like spears.

During that wait, while Turad's eyes were closed, he smelled the wolf right next to him, he felt the breath from its nostrils as it sniffed his face, and he felt its soft fur touch his neck just above the level of the sand. Slowly, cautiously, Turad opened his eyes and saw the wolf's head nestled on the ground just under his chin as it dozed, resting as one does who has just emerged from a long and taxing battle.

For a moment his eyes remained lowered toward the grave-faced wolf that hovered on the boundary between sleep and wakefulness. Then he stared up at the distant sky, muttering prayers of fear, hope, and dread. He waited a long time for the moment of perdition, for the wolf slumbered on, the exhaustion having sapped his strength. He could not get the image of Nahar out of his mind, as his face ducked and dodged the vicious onslaught of the wolf's incisors. His howling and screaming and terrible weeping still echoed in Turad's ears. Sadness and grief welled up in his heart, and tears amassed deep inside him, rose up into his throat, and formed into a flood beneath his eyelids. Turad struggled to contain them so as not to wake the sleeping wolf, but he could not hold out, and just before midnight the water began to gather in his eyes. He tried to imprison it inside the duct, tried excruciatingly to prevent the trembling tear from tumbling from his eye, but . . .

It was a decisive and terrible moment when the tear emerged. Slipping from his eye, it moved slowly down the side of his nose, slid over his dry cheek, and trickled around the edge of his mustache before it dripped suddenly, tantalizingly, onto the wolf's face. The beast awoke with a start and bared his teeth like shining swords. In a flash he had torn off Turad's left ear from the root and was chewing it in his mouth. Then he rose to his feet and withdrew a few paces into the night.

Turad's unexpected scream as the wolf snatched his left ear roused the animals and the scorpions and the snakes in the sand. The noise was enough to send the sated wolf on its way, nonchalantly munching the plucked ear like a rose in the hand of a frivolous and playful youth.

The wolf would not be gone forever. He simply had departed into the desert night to search out a place suitable for a vigilant and vicious wolf to take a nap. As soon as the whiteness of dawn appeared in the east, he would bounce down from his rocky outcrop and head back toward Shafallah Trail to kick off his day with a meal fit for the king of the wild lands, master of the ravines and wadis.

I spent the whole night shifting my body inside the sand, bending my wrists in an effort to free them from the rope with which the dogs had bound them. Those dogs of the *hajj* go to Mecca to pray when they don't possess even the decency or generosity of spirit to pardon or forgive. Aaah, I wish they'd killed us with their swords, or shot us and spared us the grisly torture. "We don't want to stain our hands with their blood when it is our intention to perform the pilgrimage," the emir of the caravan had said. What pilgrimage, when you put us slowly to death after unimaginable torment? The whole night I fought to free myself. The one who had tied me up had been in a hurry after he had spent so long on Nahar. He had tied Nahar up tightly, but the caravan was about to move off, so he tied my hands hastily as he pushed me into the hole and shoveled in the sand. Just before dawn I had freed my hands from the rope. I began to squirm about in the pit and, slowly but surely, I began to extricate myself. As the sun emerged to light up a new day, my entire right arm was already on top of the sand, and it was only a matter of moments before I had my whole body out.

I swear to Allah, I longed to see that wolf. If he'd shown up at that moment I'd have jumped on him, dragged him to the ground, and ripped his liver out. I'd have made a piss pot out of his hide, and used it every time I felt the urge. These thoughts ran through Turad's mind as he walked toward the tribes that knew him, but they did not acknowledge him and refused to believe his story. His missing ear became cause for amusement among them, and the brunt of their jokes.

That was the beginning of a life of humiliation. They insulted his dignity, his fearlessness, and his manhood. He abandoned the desert altogether and left its pastures and plains that he loved, and the trees and caves that had sheltered him and loved him back. He went into the city, whose secrets and machinations he did not know, for he was used to seeing a clearly defined enemy in front of him with whom he could join in combat like a real man. He worked as a laborer, and as a builder on the palaces at al-Marba, and then he really degraded himself, working side by side with the city's riffraff. After that he became a soldier and regained some of his self-esteem, working as a guard, first at a bank, until the bank hired a private security firm and he lost his job, and then as a guard at the entrance to a palace before he was dismissed. Then he tried begging, but at that point all he really wanted to do was go back to the desert and take by force with his right hand everything he wanted. "It's nobler to be a thief or a highwayman than to be a beggar," he said to himself.

After he'd experienced life wandering the streets, he tried to compete with the Indian and Bangladeshi car washers. He was ashamed to wash cars outside shopping malls, and he thought a parking lot at a ministry would be more respectable. As he splashed the tires of a black BMW with soapy water and scrubbed them with his brush, he glanced at the building from time to time and thought, If I were the minister of *hajj*, I'd search out the emirs of all the *hajj* caravans who've been along the Shafallah Trail, the Narrow Trail, and the Thorny Trail, and all the other routes, and I'd bury them alive in the sand. If I were the *hajj* minister I'd locate all the captains who've been involved in the trade in human beings like Tawfiq, Jawhar, Anbar, and others, and who've sold them like animals, and I'd drown them in the Red Sea.

Turad had been dreaming for a long time in the bus station waiting room when someone snatched the green file from his hand. Alarmed, he looked into the young man's face, then turned away. The face was soft and fair, his single eye wide and dark as it peered out from behind his spectacles, while his obliterated eye seemed as if it had never been created. His mustache was that of a young man in his twenties, neatly trimmed on both sides. Turad watched him as he walked away, his bag slung over his shoulder, the green file held tightly in his hand. Turad did not call to him or follow him but just contemplated his back as he disappeared into the lines of people milling around the bus whose engine had rumbled into action, and whose driver now sat behind the steering wheel.

Turad stood up and looked at his ticket, then stuffed it in his top pocket. He wrapped his red *shmagh* tightly around his face, making sure his missing left ear was well concealed. He walked sullenly between the few seats where Indian and Pakistani workers were snoozing, and he made for the door. He thought about the damn clerks in the ministry and remembered the Dutch painter van Gogh. "Why don't you lend me your ear, Van Gogh," he whispered, "so I can ward off the ridicule of the world, and you can go to Hell with your whore lover?" The street was completely still. The little snack bar on the corner had closed. In the glass telephone booth next to it, someone was talking on the phone. Three cats were asleep by the entrance to the al-Jisr grocery store. The gentle hum of the air-conditioning units compounded the silence, and the apartment windows concealed faint lights that made the passersby feel sleepy. As Turad approached the phone booth, the person inside was just hanging up and ready to leave. Turad lifted the receiver as he looked at the waiting room window and the sign of the bus company. The sound of the dial tone reminded him where he was, and he searched his pockets for a coin but couldn't find one. He noticed the edge of half a riyal resting in the slot. Mechanically he dialed the seven digits. It rang for a moment, and then at the other end a sleepy drawl: "Hello. . . . Who is it?"

". . . . ."

"Abu Loza? Where've you been, man? The guys have been asking after you."

". . . . ."

"Okay, man. The door's open. Close it behind you when you come in."

After he hung up, Turad said to himself, I'll wander around this Hell for a while before I go to Amm Tawfiq's room. Daybreak in Riyadh is the nicest time. The city's like a young woman wiping the sleep from her eyes.

Glossary

abbaya: a loose black garment that covers a woman from neck to toe. There are a variety of styles and cuts, and some are tastefully decorated or embroidered at the edges. In addition to the *abbaya*, Saudi women also wear a complete head and face covering that can be in a variety of styles. In some cases the eyes are visible between the top edge of the face veil and the bottom of the head covering, while in other cases the entire face, including the eyes, is covered.

AH: Anno Hijrae in the Islamic calendar, which dates from the *hijra* (migration), Prophet Muhammad's departure from Mecca to Medina in the year 622. The Islamic calendar is the official calendar of Saudi Arabia, although the Gregorian calendar is commonly used beside it.

al-Falaq: Daybreak, the title of verse 113 of the Koran, which is extremely potent in warding off the evil eye and is often to be found hanging in homes and shops or from the rearview mirrors of cars. It is translated by N. J. Dawood as follows: "Say: 'I seek refuge in the Lord of Daybreak from the mischief of His creation; from the mischief of the night when she spreads her darkness; from the mischief of conjuring witches; from the mischief of the envier, when he envies.'"

amm: literally, "paternal uncle"; often used as a term of respect or affection before the names of older males. The feminine equivalent is **amma**.

arta: a bush that grows in sand dunes, particularly in the deserts of Nafud and the Empty Quarter. It provides good grazing for camels and is famed for its properties as a firewood.

awshaz: also called **awsaj**; a tree with large thorns and small red berries; it can reach eight to ten feet in height. Such is the thickness of its thorns that pigeons and other similar-size birds can take refuge in it from hawks and falcons. The Badu, who call its berries "wolves' blood," believe it is inhabited by jinn, or genies, and do not chop its wood for fuel. They throw stones at it when they pass and say *"Bismillah,"* which means "in the name of Allah." Camels and goats, however, graze on its leaves, and birds eat its berries.

dahrman: fragrant wood used for cleaning teeth.

ghada: a small bush, reaching three and a half feet in height, that grows widely in central and northern Saudi

Arabia. Its wood is excellent for making fires, and burns for a long time, which has led to its disappearance in inhabited areas. Camels graze on its leaves and use it as shelter during sandstorms. The desert poets of pre-Islamic Arabia called the wolf "master of the *ghada*."

ghutra: a man's white head cloth. It is normally worn over a skullcap, with a double black band placed on top. There are a variety of styles it can be arranged in for formal and informal occasions, either allowing the edges to fall down over the shoulders or throwing them up over the top of the head.

hajj: the annual pilgrimage to Mecca.

hajji: a person undertaking the hajj.

hanshal: A local Najdi word meaning "thieves."

igal: the black band worn above the *ghutra*.

ihram: the clothes worn by pilgrims performing *hajj*, consisting of two plain white sheets or towels, one tied around the waist, the other worn over the shoulders.

kufiyya: a head cloth similar to the *ghutra* and *shmagh*. The word *kufiyya* tends to be used more in the countries of the Levant.

ma sha'allah: an expression of wonder, admiration, or disbelief, literally meaning "what Allah wills." It appears

in the Koran as the words uttered by those who enter Paradise and behold its wonders.

majlis: literally, "a place for sitting"; it is a gathering where men discuss and debate issues, or receive guests and visitors. It is also the word to describe where these activities take place, from a permanent room in a house to a tent erected temporarily for the purpose.

Moshe Dayan: renowned Israeli military commander of the 1960s and 1970s who wore an eye patch.

Muharram: the first month of the Islamic year.

riyal: Saudi unit of currency. 1 U.S. dollar = 3.75 Saudi riyals.

roashan: an ornately carved wooden balcony that is completely enclosed but allows the person standing on it to look down unseen onto the street below. They are a distinctive feature of the traditional architecture in Jeddah, the city where Tawfiq first lives when he arrives in Saudi Arabia.

samr: a tree whose branches are used as kindling and for thatching roofs. It can grow to twenty-six feet in height, and its crown is flat or umbrella-like in shape.

shafallah: a long-living bush with white or pink flowers and small edible berries, it grows to a height of about one

and a half feet. Camels are the only animals that graze on it.

shawerma: meat or chicken cooked on a rotating vertical spit. Often the meat is tightly packed in conical form around the spit, and it is rotated slowly to be carved off as it cooks. The carved strips of meat are placed in pita bread with salad, french fries, mayonnaise, and chili sauce.

sheesha: a water pipe for smoking tobacco, also known as *hookah* or *nargeela*.

shmagh: a man's head cloth, of thicker weave than the *ghutra* and usually patterned in red, though worn in the same way.

sidr: the *nabk* tree growing as high as forty feet. It has white branches and thorns. Its fruit is edible, and camels and goats graze on its leaves. The bark around the roots is used to produce a red dye. It has been said that the *sidr* menstruates like a woman because it emits a red substance from the hollows on its surface.

souk: market.

tahina: paste made from sesame seeds.

thobe: a man's garment, normally white in color and resembling a long shirt that in most cases reaches down

to the heel. Some men wear them shorter, above the ankle, which is seen as an indication of religiousness.

ya: vocative particle, used before people's names when ad-
dressing them.

I am grateful to the *Encyclopedia of Traditional Culture in the
Kingdom of Saudi Arabia* for its descriptions of the trees and
bushes.